how to be happy
on a cloudy planet

how to be happy on a cloudy planet

book 1
in the story of

Lin of Luratia

a novel by
Melanie Pahlmann

ISBN-13: 978-0615818702

Printed in the USA

Albereo Press
www.albereo.com
press@albereo.com

To the inner sanctum of sweetness

that lives in us all.

CHAPTERS

I am Lin di Ana

of the planet Luratia,

and this is the story of my life.

Koso 2293

Bisri	Misri	Kodri	Hodri	Nadri	Adri
1	2	3	4	5	6
7	8	9	10	11	12
13	14	15	16	17	18
19	20	21	22	23	24
25	26	27	28	29	30

My story begins on the 6th day of Koso 2293,

the day my life forever changed.

MOTHER

Panicked, afraid, I shouted. "Hold on, mother! Hold on!"

I kicked and kicked and kicked, swimming us furiously, desperately, back to father's boat. Mother was so weak from the murtali poison, she had little strength to give in her fight to stay alive. She couldn't swim — she could barely hold on to me — and soon she would be completely paralyzed. Even though paralysis from a murtali sting only lasts three hours, if you can't swim to safety, you will drown in the sea.

Mother's grip loosened, and she started to slip. I submerged myself so I could get under her body and lift her up on my back. I kicked hard and used my tail to propel us to the surface. Mother coughed and groaned.

"We're going to make it," I told her. "Just hold on tight."

Father shouted, "Lin! I'm throwing you a rope!"

I looked up and saw him standing on the forward side of his boat. He held up the rope high for me to see.

"Hold on, mother. Father's got us."

Mother murmured and tightened her grip around my neck.

I yelled to father, "Throw it!"

Father threw the rope, and I blinked tight to clear the water from my eyes. I needed to see the small green floater attached to the end of the rope. I needed to see where it landed.

It was a beautiful sight, the rope, moving gracefully through the air in our direction, uncoiling in a long cascade of hope. It was our lifeline, the only promise of mother's survival.

The floater landed short of us, long past my reach. Now that my eyes were clear, I saw how far we had drifted from the boat. The Casamer Sea Current was strong that day, and I could still feel it pulling us away — away from the rope, away from the boat, away from our home, away from our life.

I wanted to cry, but I knew mother would die if I did.

I kicked even harder now that the floater was bobbing on the water and I knew where to swim. I was determined to reach it, and the more determination I had, the stronger I was.

Mother held on tight enough to give me one free arm to swim with. My legs burned, my tail ached, but at least our heads were above water. The waves lifted and lowered our bodies, up and down, up and down, up and down.

"Lin, swim harder! Harder! You're almost to the rope!"

My pounding heart beat faster.

"You're almost there, Lin!"

I looked for the floater but could only see the nauseating waves that swelled and fell in every direction. Where was the floater? Would I swim right past?

Mother's grip loosened again, and I felt her body slide. I rolled under her and lifted, pulling her arm tight around my neck. The heavy weight of her body made swimming even more impossible. I wanted so much to cry. I wanted to be rescued. I wanted to be on dry land and never swim in the sea again.

"Lin! Lin! Do you see it?! Do you see it, Lin?! Do you see the floater?!" Father wouldn't stop yelling the words. "Do you see it, Lin?! The floater, in front of you! Do you see it?!"

"No!" I screamed.

I used my anger to kick harder, and it seemed to help. A high wave lifted us, and I could see the floater, bobbing close. Almost close enough to touch. On the next wave, it would be mine.

"We're almost there, mother! We're going to make it!"

As we rose up on the next wave, I reached for the floater. I felt it, I had it. I had it! I had it in my hand!

In the seconds before I tightened my grip, a wave pushed us up and took the floater with it. I reached for it, but it was gone.

Mother slid, completely this time, and slipped into the sea. In the distance, I heard father howl. It was an excruciating sound that made all my pain hurt more. I took a deep breath and dove under.

Below the surface I saw mother sinking. Her body was bent and lifeless, drifting slowly to the bottom of the sea. A silent, burning scream tore through me. I swam to her, got under her body, and pushed her up with all the strength left in me, which I feared was not enough. I had to lift all of mother's weight now, and she was nearly two of me. I forced my legs and tail to move stronger, faster. My heart pounded jarring beats of agony and love and dread.

When the last of the air left my lungs, I looked up to the water's surface. We seemed no closer from my efforts. No closer at all. I felt defeated, but I didn't want to give up. I had to save mother. I *had* to. But I also had to breathe. And to breathe, I had to let her go.

Why such a cruel choice? I was just a child.

I panicked and inhaled. It was a small amount of water, but it filled my lungs with a heavy thickness that terrified me. I let go of mother and, freed of her weight, swam easily to the surface.

"Lin! Lin! Where is she?!" were the words I heard when I reached the surface and took in a massive gulp of air.

I was relieved to be breathing, to be alive, but just as much, I'd rather have been dead. I lost her. I had her, and I lost her. And nothing could bring her back to the surface, back to life, back to us. I don't know how I stayed afloat as I treaded water, intentionally facing away from father. I couldn't bear to look at him. He was still shouting the same words, words that were meaningless now.

"She's gone!" I screamed.

I paddled around, shocked and dizzy and broken, and finally spotted the floater. I swam to it, held it tight, and looked up to see where father was. The sight of him broke my heart in a krillion pieces. He was curled up against the boat's rail on the forward side, his whole body heaving and shaking as people do when they sob uncontrollably.

I wanted to get out of the water, but I dreaded returning to the boat alone. I dreaded facing father. I was mad at him and I was afraid of him and I knew that he'd be in a volatile state. Mother always made bad moments like this all right. I wished she were here, alive and safe and with us. How would father and I ever survive this? How could we live without mother?

FATHER

Though we hardly ever spoke of it, father and I blamed each other for mother's death. I blamed him for not jumping in to save her and for taking us as far as the Casamer Current. Surely he knew the sea well enough to know there might be trouble there. He blamed me for insisting she swim when she didn't want to and for playing with such a large nest of trissilfish. When that many are nested together, they attract passengers, like the murtali waterspider that bit mother.

Despite what father may have thought, I tried desperately to save her. I loved mother, why wouldn't I? And how could he blame me when he did nothing but yell from the boat?

Of all the fathers I knew, not one of them would have been standing there, shouting hysterically, being of no help at all. But he wasn't any of those fathers, he was my father. And as much as I wished he'd saved mother, he couldn't and he didn't.

Nearly five years earlier, father lost his tail and half a leg doing battle with a deadly grangefish that got caught in his fishing net and was eating up his catch. Grangefish have large, toothy mouths and jaws that bite and don't let go. Ever since that accident, on doctor's orders, father never swam again.

I loved to swim, and mother did too. I once told father that mother and I swam enough for three people, so if he missed the joys of swimming, he could enjoy it through us.

"We're swimming for you, father!" I hollered, happy, one afternoon in the dry month of Biso as mother and I swam in the sea.

He was sitting on the fishing perch on the forward end of his boat, gazing off in some far distance.

"Father! Look, we're swimming for you!"

He glanced at me, but didn't smile. He was having no enjoyment from our happiness. He didn't even seem pleased that the cloud cover was thin that day and twice a bit of sunlight had shone through. He reached in his satchel for another sprig of kono root, spit out the one he'd just finished chewing, and turned away to gaze again at the endless stretch of sea, which glistened in certain places from tiny rays of precious sunlight.

Life by the sea makes a certain kind of person, a much different person than the cityfolk, who I felt sorry for. They had no sea to swim in, not unless they took transportation to the coast, which for them was easy enough, but when you travel to another place, it's not your home. You're a guest and you may not be welcomed.

The seafolk of Bree thought they owned the Strellin Sea. They didn't like having to share our beaches with outsiders, especially the Northerners, who spoke a different language and didn't bother to learn ours. The people of Bree didn't like different, and the Northerners who came to our beaches every dry season were as different as different can be.

That's why the people of Bree were unfriendly and took insult when the Northerners arrived with their strange city things: those small clarkon boxes that kept food hot or cold for days and days ... their stinky cheeses made from the fat of wild mountain bereks (who would eat *anything* that came out of a berek?) ... their holographic books that made imaginary people move and talk real as life in mid-air ... their halogen sticks that made light in the darkness ... and those portable clarkon domes that opened up to make a clear spherical chamber that protected anyone standing inside from rain and lightning.

Of all the strange city things the Northerners brought down to our beaches, I liked the clarkon domes the most. A book that you don't have to read, sure, has its appeal, but it can't protect you from rain and lightning. Plus, I found nothing in all the world more fascinating than amazing clarkon, which mother said was revolutionizing Luratia's way of life, everywhere but here.

Mother knew everything she knew about clarkon from her good friend Teacher Tril, whose husband traveled north to Similon every month on business. In all of Wershonia, the countries of Similon and Orilon had the most clarkon-made things. In Bree, we had none. None at all, and never would.

Until mother's death, I thought technology deprivation was the greatest tragedy I would ever suffer in life. We lived in a world of supremely great inventions, and Bree was missing out on all of them.

THE NORTHERNERS

Unlike most people, I never minded the Northern Wershonians. I rather liked them, really. It's true that they were extravagant, strange, and cultured, but if that's what culture is, I liked culture.

Every year in the dry season, when the Northerners arrived to sit on our beaches and swim in our sea, my friends Mira and Bissa and I would watch them for hours, curled up in one of the cave dwellings our ancestors carved in the tall cliff that overlooked Bree Beach. Bissa always brought her father's binoculars, and we could see with good detail the Northerners' foods and belongings, their holographic books, their moods and mannerisms, their animated way of talking, and how they were with each other.

"They sure entwine tails a lot," Bissa said once.

We laughed, not so much from embarrassment, but from the excitement of seeing something we shouldn't be seeing. The adults of Bree never entwined tails in public.

"They're in love," Mira said in a dreamy voice.

Bissa snickered. "And want all of Bree to know it."

While Mira and Bissa counted the number of tail-entwiners on the beach, I counted the number of swimmers in the sea.

"Eight," Mira said.

"Out of eighteen," Bissa grinned. "Almost half the adults are entwining tails."

They had a good laugh about it, but I was only getting angry.

"Hey Lin, what's up?" Mira asked, as a best friend would.

"I've got my own numbers," I mumbled.

"What numbers?"

"Eleven and two."

"Eleven and two what?" Bissa asked. "You have to say what the numbers mean."

"Eleven kids and two adults. Swimming."

"And that has what significance to us?"

I answered Bissa with a question: "Have you ever noticed that the Northerners let their kids swim alone?"

"No," she said, "never have."

"Look for yourself," I told her, pointing to the sea. "There's eleven kids in the water and only two adults. And the adults aren't even paying attention to them."

"Oh," Mira nodded knowingly. "This is about your father's swim rule, isn't it?"

That's exactly what it was. We had a family rule that father strictly enforced: I was not allowed to swim without an adult by my side. My friends didn't count since none of them were adults. So it was mother who usually swam with me. And on those days when she didn't want to swim when I wanted to swim, she almost always did anyway. She loved me that much.

And that's how I lost her, that horrible day, Adri, the 6th of Koso, two days before my tenth birthday — a day I asked too much of. I begged father to take us out on his boat since Adri was his only day off from fishing. I would have asked to go every Adri, but I learned that too much asking won't even get you a little of what you want. So I asked less often than I wanted, and he agreed most of the time.

But for some reason, on this particular Adri, only two days before my birthday, father said no.

"Please, please, please," I pleaded, "it's almost my birthday."

I asked again and again, like the endless squawking of a hungry fitchi seabird, the kind that made father curse from annoyment. I asked so much, he finally agreed.

Usually, when father was being stubborn with me, I would enlist mother's help in turning his position my way. But this time I didn't ask her help. She was having one of her quiet days, days when she spoke little and her body ached as if she were old. These silent spells had a name, a strange name I could never remember, so I called them quiet days. On quiet days, I knew not to trouble her.

And after all, I was nearly ten years old. It was time to be more responsible for asking of life what I wanted, all on my own.

When father finally agreed to take us out on the boat, I felt a thrilling victory. I, of my own accord and with the assistance of no one, turned the opinion of the most stubborn man in all of Wershonia. I felt triumphant and strong and a little closer to adulthood, which wouldn't come too soon, if you asked me. I was itching to grow older and have the freedom to make my own decisions. I felt like an adult trapped in a child's life and all that could release me from this prison was time.

That's why I loved my birthday. I was one year closer to me.

"Thank you, father!" I squealed.

I forgot to contain my excitement, and my tail thumped the floor.

"No thumping, Lin," father said.

I stopped thumping and turned to tell mother.

"Mother! Father's taking us out on the boat!"

It would be the last swim of mother's short, beautiful life.

THE INVENTION OF LOVEBLINKS

Loveblinks were invented by mother, inspired during a time of monumental difficulty, as are many great inventions.

Loveblinks were mother's secret way of saying "I love you" or "your father loves you" or "everything's all right" without speaking any words. In the beginning, father knew nothing about loveblinks, even though he was the one who inspired their invention, sometime in the first month after he came home from his amputation. He was angry and hurting and mean, and although he'd never stopped loving me, he acted like he had. I was too young to feel his hidden love and started to believe that he despised me. I wasn't a son, after all.

Mother insisted he loved me and tried in countless ways to reassure me, but no words were strong enough to tame my doubt. It seemed I needed something more than words, and on a afternoon as father slept, mother invented the first loveblink. It was her way of reminding me, in a way that I could feel, that father loved me as much as he ever had, no matter how unloving he may have been.

Her loveblinks were sweet and graceful and never failed to deliver the feeling of being perfectly loved and cared for. I will describe, as best I can, the experience of one of mother's loveblinks.

She can be far from you or close to you, the effect is no different. But you have to be able to see her and she you. The loveblink can't even begin until you and she are looking at each other. By this time, she has taken on an air of gentleness and serenity. If you're sensitive enough, you can feel this serenity and already you feel better or happier or assured or safe, whatever it is that's been missing.

Then the loveblink begins. Mother smiles and closes her eyes. She bows her head (my favorite part) and touches her heart with her hand. After a few tender seconds, she lifts her head, opens her eyes, and gently opens her heart-touched hand out and toward you in an offering of love.

More than any words she ever spoke, it was mother's loveblinks that got me through the nightmare of father's recovery. I once asked her why she didn't give father loveblinks. They felt so good, surely they would have helped him.

"He's not ready yet for loveblinks," she said. "He has other needs right now that no loveblink can help him with."

"But he'll be ready for them later?"

"Yes, in time, he will."

And she was right.

Being father, he wanted them a certain way. And being mother, she gladly invented a new one to suit his wishes. It happened one Hodri afternoon when his mood was fairly good and his mind was off his misery. Mother showed him a loveblink after he had finished a lunch of stufferfish and asi cakes.

"Ah, that's girl stuff," he grumbled with a smile he couldn't hide. "Let me show you how it should be done."

I was eager to see, but he wanted privacy.

"Lin," he said, "go out and check the boat. Make sure it's tied down well. I heard heavy wind this morning."

Mother shot him a scolding look and said, "If you would."

"If you would, Lin."

"Sure, father."

I hopped out of the room and out the front door. As I left I heard him yell, "No hopping indoors!"

"Jorn," mother said, "she's just a child."

"And we're her parents. She needs our guidance. She knows we mean well."

I didn't go out to the boat. I was more interested in what father thought a loveblink should be. So I quietly made my way to the window of their sleepingroom. It was half open and mostly blocked by a bryton bush planted there for privacy. I positioned myself so I could see them well and they couldn't see me at all.

"Sit next to me," father was saying to mother.

He patted the thick tichi seed cushion he had laid on day and night for the last two months. She sat down by his side and rubbed her cheek against his.

"Yes, yes," he said in a gentle voice I rarely heard from him.

She cooed in his ear, and he softly laughed. Then he picked up her hand. "Here, put your hand on my heart."

"Like this?" she asked.

"If you would," he said.

Mother smiled, her hand on his heart.

"And then," father said, "it must end with a lovebrush. To seal the love."

She leaned forward, touched her cheek to his, and caressed it in a circular motion.

He giggled. "Yes, like that."

Mother giggled too. "I've missed you, Jorn."

"I've missed you, too, Lana. I've missed you terribly."

And that's how it happened, the first reinvention of mother's famous loveblink. From that day on, father behaved better. For years, I secretly believed that mother's loveblinks had a supernatural power that healed father of his meanness and misery.

As time went on, mother found new needs and meanings for loveblinks. She took it to her teaching and loveblinked her students. Although with them, her loveblink meant nothing about love, it meant "behave", "be quiet", or "pay attention", and it involved a stern squint. It worked flawlessly she said when I asked her about it once. Father was more than skeptical. He was of the opinion that it couldn't work at all. He believed in using the "force of will" or the "power of personality" to shape up subordinates like me and his apprentices. How could a gentle, kind woman straighten up a room of misbehaving students with no words and a blink of the eyes? He thought it preposterous.

I believed mother and wanted to prove her right. I secretly talked to some of her students so I could find out for myself. I was determined to find proof so that father could see that force and will weren't the only ways to get things done.

In Nature School we learned about plants and rocks and water and weather. We were taught the practical uses of the plants and mosses, including the fantastically slimy purple-magenta seaplant known as kipper, which, among other things, was used to make the paper we wrote on in school. On a day in the month of Naso, just two months into the school year, we learned to make kipper-paper. And it was on that day that an idea struck me.

A competition.

There had been no competitions at school yet that year, and I wondered why no one had complained of it. Everyone loved the school competitions, even the townsfolk who had no children of their own. I took my idea to my best friend Mira, whose father was Director of the Lower School.

"Mira, I have an idea for a competition that I think your father should hear."

"What kind of competition?"

"Best Disciplinarian."

"A best teacher competition?"

"Right."

"I don't get it," Mira said. "The best teacher who disciplines? Don't they all discipline?"

"Not Teacher Kath, so I'm told."

We laughed at the expense of Teacher Kath, who was the brunt of many jokes, the most of any teacher in school. Teacher Kath was a nice man — too nice, perhaps — skittish and meek like the cemenot flower that closes up when you walk by.

"Poor Teacher Kath," Mira said, "he'll never marry."

"Poor Teacher Kath," I said. "It must be painful to be so unliked. If he's ever my teacher, I'll be kind to him. If there's something wonderful about him, which there has to be, I'll find it, and that's how I'll think of him."

"How high and noble of you," Mira said.

"I don't think it's high and noble. I think it's common sense. If I were Teacher Kath, I'd want at least one student to treat me kindly. It might as well be me. I've never disliked him."

Mira tapped her chin with her kipper-ink pen. "I suppose you're right. And who knows? Maybe your kindness will make him a new man. Maybe you'll rescue him from his unhappy fate."

I laughed at the thought, which I rather liked, of rescuing a grown man from anything. "Maybe," I said. "But maybe he's not unhappy. Maybe he likes being the way he is. It's hard to tell with Teacher Kath. Anyway, the competition. Listen carefully. It's not what you think. Students vote for the most unusual or most interesting way that a teacher disciplines the class."

"I like it," Mira smiled.

We spent the afternoon devising the competition categories and deciding the best way to present the idea to her father. To our surprise, he instantly approved it.

"That's quite imaginative, Mira," he said as he love-tugged her ear.

"Father," she groaned, wiggling free of the tug.

"What's the fuss?" I asked her. "I wish my father would love-tug me once in a while."

"I'm getting a little too old for that," she said.

I looked at her father and said, "Too old, you heard it."

He laughed and love-tugged my ear. I closed my eyes and savored the sensation.

"You're never too old for a love-tug," I said.

And Mira? She'd always been self-conscious of her ears. They were much shorter than they should be for a girl her age, and one bent forward a little. She was horrified that it would eventually grow even more bent and she would be a woman with one ear pointing straight up, of only medium height — making it look fat, not slender as all the men preferred — and one ear bending forward, making her look like an old, worn doll. Her father always tugged on the bent ear. Big mistake, but who was I to correct him?

"It's high time for a competition," he said. "We haven't had one yet this year."

Our competition idea passed the Competition Committee and was a smash success. Mother won by a landslide in the category we called the Most Gently Effective Disciplinarian, which of course was created precisely for her. So as not to give that away, we made a companion category, Most Menacing Effective Disciplinarian, which was hotly contested with three runners' up.

For weeks afterward, mother was congratulated everywhere she went. I started to go with her to the produce market and the merchant square and the pier where fresh fish were sold just to watch and listen as friends, acquaintances, and people we hardly knew stopped her to give their praises. In the evenings when we suppered, I would tell father of the nice things people told mother that day. He beamed with pride and always wanted to hear more. On those nights, he never grew tired of listening to what I had to say. I knew it took his mind off his pain and his troubles.

There was another personal benefit of our Most Gently Effective Disciplinarian competition. Reputation, father called it. Mother's popularity became my popularity. Because she was loved and admired, I was liked and respected. At first it bothered me to be known as Teacher Lana's daughter, as if I had no name at all. But as time went on, people began to know me as Lin, the daughter of Teacher Lana.

They were happy times, those early months of my first year of Nature School. My life was off to a good start.

Until we lost mother. It's not an exaggeration to say I almost died that day, and there have been times I wished I had.

A BODY OF FLOWERS

The people of Southern Wershonia buried their dead at sea for as long as anyone knows. The Northerners burned their dead, which I suppose they did for convenience since they had no sea.

For the funeral, it was Bree custom to put the dead one's body in a burial cloth and lay them on a wooden board beautifully decorated with colored dyes and inlaid drae shells. Family and friends circle around the burial cloth, which is fully closed up so that only the shape of the body can be seen.

When a deceased is not present for their own funeral, a burial cloth is still used, but the cloth lies fully opened, its edges draping over the sides of the wooden board. Everyone who gathers brings with them a flower and lays it on the open cloth, making a whole new body for the deceased — a body of beautiful, fragrant flowers. The more people in attendance, the more flowers there are, and the more vibrant the color and lovely the scent.

My father's sister, Aunt Tala, counted the number of people who came to mother's funeral: 278. Father was sure it was an all-time record for a Bree funeral, but his curmudgeon friend, Califer Crigs, disagreed. He thought more were at *his* wife's funeral, who had died a few years back when a mudslide dumped their house in the sea and her along with it.

About mother, this we knew for sure: there had never been more flowers placed on a burial cloth in all the years Elder Evig and his wife had been conducting funerals.

They were standing beside me when I heard her say to him, "Oh dear, we have a problem. There are too many flowers, what shall we do?"

"Hmm," he said, stroking his chin.

I instantly saw a solution, a good one, I thought. "I have an idea," I turned and told them.

Elder Evig's wife smiled at me, her eyes more kind and sparkly than I remembered, though this may have been the closest to her I'd ever stood.

"You have an idea about the flowers?" she asked.

"Yes. What if father and I and the two of you hold up the corners of the cloth?"

"Very good," said Elder Evig, nodding his approval.

"Indeed," said his wife. "Shall we ask your father, or would you prefer to?"

"Would you ask him, Madam Evig?"

"Of course." She glanced at the growing pile of flowers and said, "We should hurry, but first, Lin, tell me how you are."

"I miss mother terribly," I told her. "My Aunt Tala has been staying with us, so we're eating well and being taken care of. But still...." I bit my lip to keep from crying.

"You will see, Lin, that your mother's love and goodness will always live on in your heart, even now and especially when you miss her the most. If you take some time alone and roam the inner space of your heart and feel your love for her, you will find her there." She smiled again. Her eyes glistened so brightly I thought golden tears would fall from them.

"Thank you, Madam Evig, I like that. I like that a lot."

She took my hand and said, "Let's go now."

Father looked surprised about the idea she whispered in his ear. Elder Evig approached him from the other side and whispered something too. Father nodded and smiled and stepped to the headward end of the burial cloth, the place where Elder Evig always stood at a funeral. When we were all in place, each holding a corner of the burial cloth, Elder Evig nodded, and together we lifted our corners, making a rectangular bowl that was now fit to hold the remaining flowers.

Many of the onlookers quietly commented on the unusualness of this. Some were whispered in my ear:

"Isn't that lovely? An over-abundance of flowers."

"Do you see how well liked your mother was?"

"You must be proud to know how much we admired your mother."

They whispered in father's ear too. Some made him smile.

Mira was right, it was an especially beautiful funeral.

When the last flower was laid, Elder Evig's wife and I drew and tied the corners together. It was an exceptionally fat burial cloth, bulging oddly in some places, and large enough to hold two grown people and a child my age.

Elder Evig returned to the headward end and gave the closing funeral rite. Mother's body of flowers was hoisted onto the boat, and father and I and Elder Evig and the boat captain sailed out to sea. Nothing was said until the boat anchored.

We all watched as mother's body of flowers was gently lowered into the sea, weighted by two bags of rocks affixed to each end of the burial cloth.

"Goodbye, mother," I said out loud, my voice shaky from crying. "I'll love you always."

I looked at father. He stood motionless, jaw clenched, fighting tears, staring at the tiny air bubbles that danced on the surface of the murky water, which had now taken her body of flowers fully from our sight.

I wanted to say, "I love you, father," but I was afraid.

"How messed up is that?" I later confided to Mira. "I was afraid to tell father I loved him."

"It's a perfectly normal thing to say," she said.

"Especially right there on the funeral boat."

"Have you tried telling him about it?"

"No," I said, "but maybe I will."

"Maybe you should."

I thought about telling father and doubted that I ever would.

"Is your father crying about your mother?" Mira asked me.

"Yes. A lot, I think. Sometimes I hear a muffled, wailing sound coming from his sleepingroom in the middle of the night. He's crying, and he's hiding it from me, I can tell."

"My father sure would."

"Some nights I can't fall asleep at all," I said. "When that used to happen, I'd go wake mother. She never minded. She'd curl up with me on my sleepingcushion and rub my ears and whisper a story about a girl who loved to sleep. She always made everything better. I don't know how I'm going to live without her."

"If I lost my mother, I'd be a wreck of a person," Mira said. "And you didn't just lose your mother, you lost your father."

"You're right."

"You lost your home life. All you have is your Aunt Tala."

"And you."

"And me," Mira said, "but I can't come live with you."

"That'd be fun."

"What would be fun is for you to live with us."

I smiled at her, wishing, wishing, wishing for the impossible. "Living with you and your parents? That'd definitely be more fun." I imagined living at Mira's and only got more sad. I knew it would never happen. "Life's so unfair, Mira. And I'm too young to do anything about it."

"What's unfair about life is that some people seem to get all the good luck and some get all the bad."

"And then there's a bunch of people in the middle who only get a little of both."

"You're right," Mira said. "Maybe I'll write a story about that, a story about luck."

"You know what's most unlucky of all, beside mother dying?"

"That your tenth birthday was ruined?"

"No," *but how odd,* I thought, *I don't even care about that now.* "No, not that. She was going to take me to the World Library."

Mira's eyes opened wide. "Out to the Embassy Island?"

"Yes," I nodded. "Just a few days before mother died, she promised me."

"Really?"

"Really."

"That's so cruel," Mira said.

"Tell me about it."

"How'd you convince her?"

"It was her idea."

Mira nodded. "She really loved you, Lin."

"I know. More than father."

"He loves you differently."

"He doesn't love me enough to take me, I'll tell you that. He hates modern things."

"What about your Aunt Tala? Would she take you?"

"I don't know. Maybe. But the problem is convincing father to let me go. Mother was so good at talking him into things."

A fire of anger burned in me. I was more than sad that mother had died, I was angry. Not at mother, she was an innocent victim. I was angry that I begged her to go swimming and that I couldn't save her and that she was bit by a murtali in the first place. Life would be so much better for everyone if we didn't have to worry about dying from a murtali sting or getting your leg chomped off by a grangefish. Why did mean, dangerous creatures have to exist at all? That was a fact of life I couldn't understand.

But I will say this, the existence of mean, dangerous creatures did help me better understand meanness in people. It seemed that every person was similar to one kind of animal or insect or bird, one more than any other. Mother was like the white cerenum lovebird. Father was like the big brown grandis, the strongest of all the forest animals — ferocious, loud, loyal, and protective of his clan. Aunt Tala was like the reducti, not that she's a rodent, but they did have similar character traits — fussy, bossy, and organized. And Jabe di Groot, the meanest boy in my class at school, was like a murtali — small, spindly, and vicious, whose poisonous words could leave a person paralyzed for hours.

I didn't think Jabe was mean because he wanted to be, I thought he was mean because he was born with the character of a murtali waterspider. And how much of our character do we have any real choice about when we're young? It's not until we get older that we can change our character and make it better. That's how it seemed to me.

And it was true, I didn't care that my tenth birthday was completely ignored because of mother's death. I only cared that I was one year older.

KODRI 3 KOSO

"There you are, Lin."

Mother was radiant, standing silhouette in the arched portal that connected the front entrance of our living quarters with the sittingroom. Ordinarily I would have gone to market with her, but the day was Kodri and the month was Koso, and every Kodri in Koso mother and her teacher friends liked to meet at market to talk about the upcoming year and share stories of the Freedom Months — the three months in between school years when no classes were held at all.

"You look happy, mother," I said as I followed her into the kitchen, towing one of her stuffed slingbags.

"I am," she said. "I have something wonderful to tell you."

"We're getting a pet adibadi?"

I slid the slingbag to her feet, helped her lift it to the cooking table, and waited to hear if we were going to be the first family in Bree to own an adibadi.

She laughed and kissed me on the head. "No, it's better than that."

Better than an adibadi? What could be better than having your own adibadi, if what they said was true? — that they stand almost tall as a man, understand the meaning of the words you speak, and do whatever you tell them to do, and sweetly? Legend had it that an adibadi could be trained to do nearly every kind of chore: clean dinner plates, sweep the floors, carry heavy slingbags, sew up torn raincapes, and de-bug the garden, which is an easy chore for them since they just eat the bugs. Every child old enough to do chores dreamt of owning a pet adibadi.

But adibadis were hard to come by. They were native to the Continent and expensive to transport to faraway places like Southern Wershonia, especially Bree, which was the most faraway of faraway places, the furthest removed from the major import routes.

That was my secret nickname for Bree: "furthest removed" — furthest removed from modern technology, furthest removed from the big cities, and furthest removed from the Continent, the most modern country in the world. Bree was so far removed, no sub-orbital airbuses ever traveled here, not even overhead on their way to other places.

The satellite broadcasts that constantly poured out of the sky still didn't reach us. The Bree Committee of Technology had seen to that. I called them the Committee of No Technology, since they were clearly against anything modern.

The Committee of No Technology was a group of 13 elders, none of them under 80 years old. What did they know about technology? Why did they get to decide what technology we should and shouldn't have? The only great decision they'd made in the last 50 years was to approve the installment of the energy relay dish that received the free electricity that the satellites of the Continent collected from the sun and beamed down to the world for everyone to use. That had been the biggest technological improvement in Bree ever, but even that decision wasn't motivated by an interest in technology. The Committee of No Technology approved the energy relay dish not to modernize Bree, but to save money. As father said, "Who in their right mind would say no to free electricity?"

"What could be better than an adibadi?" I asked mother.

"I'm going to take you to the World Library. They have clarkon there. We'll go before school starts."

A joy explosion burst inside me and about knocked me off my feet. "The World Library? On the Embassy Island?"

"Yes," she laughed.

I wrapped my arms around her and squeezed hard. Unlike father, mother never exaggerated and never made promises she didn't mean to keep. Whenever I questioned the truth of what she said, she always replied, "If it weren't true, I wouldn't have said it."

"We're really going! Thank you, mother! I'm so happy! So, so happy!"

"I'm eager to go myself," she said. "I've always been interested in the World Library."

"Really? You never talk about it."

"Talking is not the same as doing," mother said. "I haven't had the opportunity to go, so there's been no point in talking about it."

"Have you ever mentioned it to father?"

"Yes, once, long ago, before you were born."

"What'd he say?"

"That he had absolutely no interest in such things."

"Ouch."

"Yes," she laughed, "it stung a little. But it wasn't so important to me that I felt the desire to press him on it. It wasn't worth fighting for. Other things were, but not that."

"What other things?" I asked.

"In those days, creating a close and happy marriage with your father."

"You had to fight for that?"

"A happy marriage requires effort, no matter who you are."

"I can't believe we're going."

"Before the school year starts, we'll go."

"Are you doing this for my birthday?"

"I'm doing this because I love you." She kissed me again on the top of my head, in the space between my ears, my favorite place to be kissed.

Only three days later, mother went swimming with me in the sea — not because she wanted to, but because she loved me.

In a matter of three days, I had the best day and the worst day of my entire life. One day my ultimate wish was granted, and three days of joy later, the most precious person I had ever loved was taken from me.

And now that mother was gone, how would I ever get to the World Library? We hadn't even told father yet, and I had big doubts that he'd approve of the idea, especially now during his time of grief.

My only hope was Aunt Tala.

AUNT TALA

Aunt Tala came to live with father and I the day after mother's death, exactly four weeks before the first day of school. I liked Aunt Tala well enough if I didn't see her very often, but all day long for four weeks was going to be too much. I secretly wished she would tire of me so we could get someone else to take her place.

Aunt Tala was a busybody and liked to look at mother's things, which irritated me and made it more difficult to like her. I wanted to tell her that these things were not hers and that she had no right to pick them up and ask me questions about where they came from or if we would be giving them away. But I kept quiet about it. Aunt Tala had a temper. She was a lot like father, she could be stern and mean. Mira said she's sure that's why Aunt Tala hadn't married. She once said of Aunt Tala, "She's not a pleasant woman."

She was, though, a very good cook. A better cook than mother. And although I had no interest in cooking, I knew it was a way I could get through to Aunt Tala's inner sanctum of sweetness. I believed that everyone had sweetness deep inside of them, even the gruff ones like father and Aunt Tala and Jabe di Groot, the meanest boy in school. You just had to help them find it or, with a little cleverness, make the right conditions for it to naturally shine through.

"Do you know what, Aunt Tala?" I asked one night at dinner.

"What, Lin?"

"You're the best cook I know."

She swallowed her truly delicious pillowfish soup and smiled at me. A faint flicker of sweetness was already shining through.

"Why, thank you, Lin. That's a nice thing to say."

"I'm not just saying it, it's true. If it wasn't true, I wouldn't have said it."

Father shot me a look. Was he angry at me for borrowing mother's words or did it make him sad to hear them?

"Would you teach me how to cook?" I asked her. "I could be your helper. I could be your kitchen adibadi."

Father coughed and almost spit some soup across the table at Aunt Tala. Fortunately for both of them, he was quick with his diningcloth and caught it in time. Aunt Tala didn't even flinch. She had no idea that she had just been rescued from a highly awful incident.

"Kitchen adibadi," father said as he nodded a laugh. "That was funny, Lin."

I bathed in his praise and silently praised him in return for laughing for the first time since mother died. Father loved humor and was never miserly about savoring something funny when he heard it. I was sensing a faint flicker of *his* sweetness shining through. This was all going very well.

Aunt Tala smiled at me. "A kitchen adibadi?" she said. "Sounds good to me."

Victory bubbled in my belly. Maybe Aunt Tala wasn't as difficult as I thought her to be.

"Why don't we begin tomorrow, Aunt Tala? I could help you shop at the market."

Aunt Tala wiped an eye with her diningcloth and looked at father. "Jorn, you've raised a fine daughter. Well behaved and helpful."

Father squinched his eyes and gave a single nod. "Yes, she is."

"Does that mean yes, Aunt Tala? We can start tomorrow?"

"Yes, we'll go to market in the morning. And, Lin," she said in a voice so sweet I feared there was a catch.

"Yes, Aunt Tala?"

"There's something you can teach me. I want you to show me what foods and flavors your father likes and doesn't like."

"That'd be good," father said.

We didn't make it to the market until late morning, not right after breakfast as we had planned. An early morning storm had blown in, and we woke before daylight to the screeching blare of the lightning siren, which always went off when the animal sentinels got anxious. For almost five hours everyone had to stay home on storm alert while rain pounded our rooftops and lightning seared the sky. By late morning the normalcy signal sounded, and we were free again to leave our homes.

It would be a far stretch to say that Aunt Tala and I had had fun at the market, but we did have a nearly continuous conversation, mostly relating to father's food preferences. I didn't once mention clarkon or the World Library. I'd grown old enough to know about the timing of things and when it was the right time to bring up a sensitive subject and when it wasn't. Meandering the noisy market with its endless distractions was not the time or place to bring up one of the most important questions I may ever ask in my life.

We brought home three slingbags full of father's favorite foods and officially began cooking meals together with me as her apprentice and cleaning slave. I learned three things as her apprentice: first, I was not a natural born cook; second, Aunt Tala had much less patience than me; third, I had much more patience than I thought.

The market was a terrible place to ask a monumentally important question, and so was the kitchen when cooking was going on. When Aunt Tala and I cooked together, I never brought up the World Library. When Aunt Tala made up her mind, it was difficult to persuade her otherwise. The way I saw it, I had one chance to convince her, so it had to be the right chance at the right time.

The patience Aunt Tala's obstinance forced me to bear was made easier by those occasional moments when I got through to her inner sanctum of sweetness. One in particular happened on an Adri in Hoso, two weeks after the start of school.

"Father never used to work on Adri's," I told her. "Never."

Aunt Tala rubbed my ears with a reassuring tenderness and said, "Your father works every day because it helps him get his mind off his loss. Be patient with him. In time, this will all pass. It's going to be a difficult adjustment, but you *will* adjust, and this time of grief will be a far memory." She love-tugged my ear. "You'll see."

I was suddenly overcome with missing mother, and I began to cry. Aunt Tala held me in her arms and gently scratched behind my ears as I cried and cried and cried. It was the first time since mother died that I felt mothered.

After that day, I cried in Aunt Tala's lap whenever my sadness got too big. It wasn't the same as crying in mother's arms, but it was nurturing, and I was desperate for nurturing. She seemed to like it too, especially when I asked her questions, which she usually answered quite well. She was smart, it turned out, and knew more things about the world than father, perhaps more than mother too. And there I found my way in.

"Aunt Tala?"

"Yes, Lin?"

"Do you know what clarkon is?"

"Yes, the solar satellites are made of clarkon."

"You know about the solar satellites?"

"Yes, have you learned about them in school?"

"No, not yet. I'm still in Nature School. What do you know about the satellites?"

"Well, there are two of them. Forton and Alteron. Forton is the smaller one. It has a large telescope that can see far into the universe."

"Have you seen pictures of the universe?"

"Some. I've seen the double star Albereo."

"I have too," I said, "in a book of space that Teacher Tril lent mother. It's so beautiful, isn't it? The blue star and the golden star."

"And they're in close proximity," Aunt Tala said. "Did you know that Albereo is only 8 light years from here? If we didn't have cloudy skies, the stars of Albereo would be enormous bright-shining jewels in the dark sky of night."

I was impressed with her knowledge of astronomy and overjoyed for our kindred love of space and technology. Had I underestimated Aunt Tala all these years? Had she always been an interesting person and I didn't know because I never asked her the right questions?

I thought of a story mother once told me.

"Imagine a man," she said, "a mean-looking man with a large stick in his hand. He's snarling and vicious and ready to strike. What do you think of him?"

"I think he's a horrible person and should be put in jail."

"And why jail?"

"Because he's dangerous and mean. He's going to hurt someone with his stick."

"All right," mother said. "Now I'm going to tell you more about this man. Standing behind him are two young children. In front of him is a big, hungry grandis who hasn't eaten in days and is intent on having these children for lunch. What do you think of this man now?"

"He's a wonderful man. He's protecting the children."

"He doesn't belong in jail?"

"No, he belongs with his family."

"And what changed your mind?"

"Seeing the children."

"Do you think there's a lesson in this story?"

I thought about it, and there clearly was. "You shouldn't judge a person until you know something about them."

"That's right, Lin, that's exactly right." She kissed me on the head and hugged me tight.

Aunt Tala was like this man in the story. I didn't know her until she came to live with us. Short holiday visits aren't enough to know someone well, not if you don't have a meaningful conversation with them, which I'd never had with her until now.

Despite her stranger qualities, I truly liked getting to know Aunt Tala better. Overall, she was a good person — intelligent and learned and a true lover of technology.

The light of optimism was beginning to shine on the dark places inside me where sadness and hopelessness lived.

I was beginning to feel optimistic about going to the World Library. I was beginning to feel optimistic about surviving life without mother. I would never stop missing her, but I believed life could get better even so.

The Incident with Jabe di Groot

The sea was rough and the waves were high — so high that on the downswell, I feared the sea would swallow me. But the upswell always lifted me again, high enough to see the far edge of the horizon.

I didn't know how I got here, and I didn't know how to get back to shore. On the upswells, I had looked at least once in every direction, but saw no trace of land. I saw no boat, no buoy, no driftwood, nothing solid I could hold on to. I was alone and isolated in a part of the Strellin Sea I didn't recognize. I feared I had drifted as far as the ocean itself. Judging by the size of the waves, that was entirely possible.

How would I ever get home?

I knew this much: treading water was getting me nowhere. I had to choose a direction and swim. Then the idea struck me: look beneath. I took a deep breath and dove below the surface. All the typical fish were swimming nearby, mostly in small schools. In a far distance, I saw a trissilfish nest, a white fuzzy mass hovering close to the water's surface. It was the most massive nest I'd ever seen, massive enough to fully hold my weight. I swam to it with the hope it had no unfriendly passengers.

When I reached the nest, I inspected it for safety, finding nothing toothy or poisonous. I positioned my feet, drew my body up to a standing position, and lifted my head above water.

I surveyed the sea, praying for anything that would get me back home. But not a single solid anything was in sight. I was trapped in the vast, empty sea.

And then I felt it — *Ouch!* — a small but searing pinch on my right foot. *Ouch!* Then another. *OUCH!* Then more, many more. I breathed in deep and plunged my head underwater, bending down low to get a good look. I thought I'd pass out from the horror I saw. An army of murtali was feasting on my legs and feet.

Then I screamed and woke up.

"Lin? ... Lin?" The voice was soft and sweet and not Aunt Tala's. "Lin, are you all right?"

My bleary eyes brought the face of the voice in focus. There were other faces too, gawking faces, curious and laughing and unkind.

A sickening dread came over me. I wasn't at home this time, curled up on my sleepingcushion. I was on the beach, in Nature School. I was safe from the murtali, but I thought I'd die from embarrassment. I'd fallen asleep in school before, but I'd never had a nightmare there. I never had any nightmares before mother died. Never. Now I had them two or three times a week.

"Lin, are you all right?" Teacher Hana was kneeling next to me, her yellow-green eyes the color of mother's — the exact color and the same shape. I couldn't stop looking at them. "Lin?" She gently took hold of my hand. I could see the concern in her face. I could feel that she cared about me.

"I think she's gone mad," I heard someone say. I knew the voice. It was Jabe di Groot.

A rumble of laughter rose up around me. I wondered who had laughed and who didn't. I wanted not to care, but I did.

Teacher Hana turned toward Jabe and said loud for everyone to hear, "Jabe, that is *not* acceptable behavior. I want to see you after class."

"Yes, Teacher Hana," he mumbled.

Teacher Hana turned back to face me, but my eyes were now on Jabe. He made an ugly face at me and mouthed some words I couldn't decipher. *Great.* Now Jabe was mad at me because he was scolded in front of everyone for insulting me. Even though I'd never been a victim of Jabe's verbal assaults, I always pitied the ones who were. Jabe never hit anyone, but you don't have to inflict physical pain to really hurt a person.

"Lin, are you all right, sweetheart?"

I looked into Teacher Hana's eyes and let the sound of the word wash over me.

"Yes, I'm all right. It was a bad dream. I'm sorry I fell asleep."

"You're quite shaken up," she said.

Teacher Hana looked up at the dim glow of the sun in the cloud-covered sky. She was one of the few teachers who could tell time that way and was the most accurate among them. She took first place in a competition two years ago. It was called the Best Time-Teller Based on the Position of the Sun.

She whistled and yelled at my schoolmates, "Class is almost over, everyone! Let's end early today!"

They cheered and squealed and leapt to their feet, running in all directions.

"Thanks, Lin!" I heard someone say.

"Yeah, thanks, Lin!"

"You should have more nightmares," said a boy named Krin, "but try to fall asleep earlier next time!"

"Krin," said Teacher Hana, her eyes still on mine, "I know that was you. And Jabe, I want to see you now."

Jabe had actually calmed down a little this year, due mostly or completely to the influence of Teacher Hana. He liked her and he always did as she told. When she said to him "I want to see you now", he was already walking toward her. He respected her authority, and I believed that if he had a few more years with Teacher Hana, he might have changed his ways.

The sound of joy was dissipating, and this spot of the beach where we gathered for Nature School was empty now except for Teacher Hana, me, Jabe, Mira, and a couple of schoolmates who stayed to play in the surf. For the first time since I'd waken from my nightmare, I saw Mira. She was sitting on a nearby rock, writing in a hand-bound kipper-paper notebook she made herself. She looked up, saw me, and smiled. I knew she was waiting for me, my great and loyal friend.

"I'm sorry, Teacher Hana," I heard Jabe say from where he stood behind me.

I could see by his reflection in her eyes that he looked directly at Teacher Hana as he said it. Mean little Jabe di Groot apologized without being told to. *He really is improving.*

"Thank you, Jabe," Teacher Hana said, "although the apology really belongs to Lin. What you said about her was unkind and unnecessary. Can you feel the truth of that?"

"Yes, Teacher Hana," he said in a quiet voice.

"Will you apologize to Lin?"

"I'm sorry, Lin."

I didn't say anything. I couldn't even see him, and it bothered me.

"Jabe," she said, "I want you to tell me what just happened here. Be like a newsman, reporting the facts. Describe to me the events, from the beginning, that led to the action for which you are now apologizing."

"I want to see Jabe," I whispered to Teacher Hana.

She took his hand. "Come over here, Jabe, so we can all see each other. There, that's good. Now, tell me what happened. And then we'll all go home."

"I was minding my own business," Jabe said, his eyes to the sky, "listening to our lesson on shelled animals and the many functions of the exoskeleton." He paused, as if to let that statement linger in Teacher Hana's mind and register in her the thought, *Jabe di Groot was paying superb attention to my lesson today, what an excellent student.* She said nothing, nor did she smile, she just patiently waited for Jabe to get on with it.

He let out a nervous cough and continued: "Then all of a sudden, I heard a loud scream. It startled me and disrupted the whole class. It was so startling and unusual that we all laughed."

Teacher Hana cracked a smile. "And you said...?"

Jabe squirmed and sighed and then gave in. "I said 'I think she's gone mad.' I said it because I wanted to break the tension in the class by saying something funny."

"Sounds like your motive was noble and altruistic," Teacher Hana said, "for the good of the whole class."

"Yes, ma'am."

"Do you think it did some good?"

"Everyone laughed."

"Ah," she smiled. "And that laughter was good medicine for an uncomfortable moment?"

"Yes, Teacher Hana. I hoped it was."

"And did the laughter benefit *you* in any way?"

"Well...." Jabe was caught in a trick question. His tail twitched nervously. His ears too. He was hating every moment of this. And I was hating him less. I wasn't hating him at all, in fact. Him hating this moment did all my hating for me. And in that place where my hatred for Jabe burned just minutes ago, I felt a small, tender sadness for him. This surprised me, in a happy way. In the middle of this awful incident, my inner sanctum of sweetness shined a ray of kindness and put friendliness in my thoughts.

"Does it make you happy to make people laugh?" Teacher Hana asked Jabe after a long silence.

"I suppose so."

"I feel wonderful when I make someone laugh," she said.

Jabe had no response to that. He was staring at the ground, stewing in humiliation.

"Do you know what point I'm trying to get at, Jabe?"

"I think maybe I don't."

"Intention," she said. "The intention of your statement. Did you say it to intentionally hurt Lin?"

"No."

"I believe you, Jabe. I believe you didn't intend to hurt Lin." She spoke the words like a kind mother, smiling as she did. "I also don't believe your intentions were altruistic. I have a pretty good sense of your true intention in saying what you said, Jabe, but if *you* know, I would rather hear it from you."

Teacher Hana was completely patient and her eyes were sweet and soft. It was as though she was holding him, but without arms. She was holding him with love and kindness. I almost cried myself.

Finally, Jabe spoke. "I know what my intention was, Teacher Hana. I wanted to get a laugh. It was a ripe circumstance for a joke, and I couldn't stop myself."

"Is there anything you would like to say to Lin?" she asked.

I looked at Jabe. He looked at me. He wasn't glaring, not an enemy glare, not even an angry glare. His meanness was gone.

"I'm sorry I hurt your feelings," he said. "I really didn't mean to."

"Thanks, Jabe," I said. "I know you didn't mean to hurt me. It could've been anyone who fell asleep and had a nightmare. I won't take it personally."

He smiled a smile he couldn't hide. "Don't worry," he said to me. "Don't worry about your nightmares. They're never real. I have them too sometimes. So did my older brother. But he doesn't have them anymore. I think we grow out of them."

"I hope so. Thanks, Jabe. Thanks for saying that."

Teacher Hana smiled and nodded her pride in him. "I'm very proud of you, Jabe, for taking the time to speak with Lin and I. It was an act of respect toward Lin, and it was an act of self-respect toward youself. I see a fine young man in you." She motioned with her hand. "Go now, you're excused. We'll see you in school tomorrow."

"All right, Teacher Hana." He turned to go and then turned back around. "Bye, Lin, see you tomorrow."

"See you tomorrow, Jabe."

Before I even thought to thank her, I asked Teacher Hana a burning question. "How did you do that? If I believed in superstition, I'd think you have a magic power."

Teacher Hana laughed. "Well, it is a power, but it's not magic."

"What is this power?"

"I would be happy to tell you another time. It's *you* I'd like to talk about first."

Was I in trouble? "I'm sorry for falling asleep," I said.

"There's no need to apologize, Lin. You've done nothing wrong."

Except cause my mother's death. But I would never tell her that. My secret would stay with Mira.

"Are you having frequent nightmares?" Teacher Hana asked.

"More than I used to. Well, I used to have none, so that's not saying much. Two or three times a week, I guess."

"Are they deeply terrifying dreams? Are you in danger?"

I thought about all the different nightmares I'd had and told her about one where I'm in the sea with mother and father and they'd both been stung by murtali waterspiders. I'm trying to save them, and I manage to keep them from drowning. But it's impossible to swim them to the boat. When I have father up, mother would slip. When I bring mother up, father would slip. I'm strong enough to swim one of them to safety, but not both, and I'm angry that I have to choose between them. My anger grows so fierce, I'm suddenly endowed with super-Luratian power. I take them under my arms and leap out of the water with a tremendous force that propels the three of us through the air and onto father's boat. Mother and father are weak from the murtali poison, but they're safe and they survive.

"That's my favorite of the nightmares," I said to Teacher Hana. "It turns out well."

"This nightmare is not as frightening as the others?" she asked.

"No."

"Are these recurring dreams?"

"Recurring?"

"Do you have them repeatedly?"

"Yes."

"Have you been talking to anyone about this? Your aunt or your father or Elder Evig's wife?"

"Elder Evig's wife?"

"Yes, she's an excellent listener and counselor. Have you been talking to no one?"

"No."

"No one at all?"

"No."

"Would you like to?"

"I would talk to Elder Evig's wife. She's always been nice to me."

Teacher Hana looked down to the ground and drew a long breath. "Even though your mother and I were very close friends, it's not my place to directly intervene in your welfare. But I'm deeply concerned for you. It's important that you not keep these nightmares to yourself. Do you understand why that might be true?"

"I believe it's true," I said. "I think I'll like talking to someone about my dreams. I like talking about them with you."

"And your aunt, do you feel comfortable telling her about your nightmares?"

"Yes, she knows about them. They've woken her up a few times. Father sleeps right through. He doesn't know at all. I don't really want him to."

"He doesn't have to know as long as someone does." Teacher Hana took my hands and squeezed them lightly. "Will you promise me that you will talk to your aunt about the frightening dreams?"

"Sure."

"You don't have to tell her the details of the dreams. Tell her how they make you feel. She needs to know how terrifying they are. And then, if you like the idea of talking to Elder Evig's wife, tell your aunt that too."

"All right."

I decided in that moment that I would.

As Mira and I walked home, I told her everything that happened.

"There's ten stories in that," she said.

"Everything's a story to you, Mira."

"Life's nothing but stories," she said, "all weaving in and out of each other, intertwined like the trissilfish in a trissilfish nest."

"I like it when a sad story turns into a happy story. Like today, I had a bad nightmare in public and was cruelly laughed at. But then, Jabe and I became friends."

"We'll see how long that lasts."

"I have faith in Jabe," I said, "as long as Teacher Hana's there to be a good influence. If she were his mother, he'd be a completely different person."

"Agreed. Too bad she's already married. She could marry your father and be your mother."

I saw in my mind the wedding of father and Teacher Hana. I saw her living with us. Aunt Tala was gone and Teacher Hana was there in her place — in mother's place — cooking in the kitchen, serving dinner, reading to father books about fish and the ocean currents, whispering sweetnesses in his ear, talking calmly with him about his difficulties with people, and giving him good ideas in such a way that he thought the ideas were his.

"No," I said to the idea of their marriage. "It wouldn't work, even if she loved him the way mother did."

Even though Teacher Hana would have been a quite perfect mother, her marriage to father didn't make me happy.

I missed Aunt Tala.

LOVING THE UNLOVABLE

Nothing had worked.

First I asked nicely. Then Aunt Tala asked nicely, as nicely as she could. Then Aunt Tala asked less nicely. Then she threatened not to cook anymore. As much as father loved her cooking, his answer was the same: "I'm not going! Leave me alone!"

Aunt Tala turned away from the locked door of father's sleepingroom and threw up her hands. "I give up," she said. "I wish him well in his misery."

Grandmother Min arrived on the scene and tapped lightly on the door. "Jorn, honey, I know you don't care for Elder Evig's service, but try to find in yourself a reason to go with us. It will be good for you to get out and be around people who care about you. I happen to know your old school friend Pischa will be there. He's in Bree this week."

"Never liked that old fool," father mumbled.

"Jorn, please, go with us. You need the support of your community now more than ever."

"Don't like 'em, don't need 'em. Just leave me in peace."

"But that's the problem, Jorn. You have no peace. If you think that sitting alone at home will give you peace, you're fooling yourself."

"Aaahhhh, good sun!" father bellowed. "How often must I repeat myself? I'm not going! I work hard five days a week! Adri's my only day to rest! Lana understood that, why won't you?"

Father had a point, I thought. I buried my face in my hands and entertained the notion of slipping away unnoticed and going to service with Mira and her family.

I heard another knock on father's door.

"Jorn?"

It was Grandfather Daun, who joined in on the coaxing.

"My family's gone mad!" I told Mira when I reached her house. I left while no one was looking and found her sitting on the flat-top tree stub in her front yard, writing in her kipper-paper notebook.

"Want to go to service," I asked, "the two of us?"

"Sure," she said. She hopped off the stub and gave a shout to her parents through their kitchen window, "Mother, Father, I'm going on with Lin!"

"Be careful!" ... "See you there!" I heard them say.

"Your family *is* mad," Mira said after I told her the whole story.

"And getting madder. Missing mother is enough grief already," I said. "I don't know how much longer I can put up with their childish arguments. I think they'd rather fight than solve their problems. It's aggravating to live with."

"It's kind of ironic," Mira said. "Fighting about going to Elder Evig's service. Isn't that defeating the purpose?"

"You're right. Even if they manage to drag father out of his self-pity and get him to service, you know they're going to sit there furious and fuming, every one of them."

"While Elder Evig gives a talk on love and tolerance."

I laughed. "And there's my family, stewing in their anger, ignoring the love Elder Evig's talking about. That's the problem with arguments and anger. You have to give up love for them."

Mira shook her head. "It makes no sense. Why give up love for anger? Anger always feels awful. And what feels better than love?"

"Nothing," we said in unison.

"Do we know these things as kids," Mira said, "and then forget them when we grow up?"

"I think some kids have forgotten them already."

We giggled and said in one voice, "Jabe di Groot."

Mira love-tugged my ear. "I love it when we do that."

"Say the same thing at the same time?"

"Yes," she said, "I think it's the mark of a great friendship."

"Me too." I love-tugged Mira's ear, the good one. "I think your father's one of the best fathers around," I said, "but every time I see him love-tug your ear, it's always the bent one."

"I know," she said. "I think he's trying to straighten it out, even though that would never work, even if he did it every day. I know that for a fact. I asked Doctor Taal about it once."

"Does it bother you that he does it?"

"Yes and no," she said. "It reminds me that I'm defective, which is painful, but I know he does it because loves me."

"He does love you," I said, "it's obvious. My father loves me, I know he does, but it's not obvious. I have to remind myself."

"I wonder if he's going to show up at service today," Mira said.

"Let's sit in the back so we can see."

"Sounds good."

We laughed all the way there, belly laughs, real and happy-making. I was having a better day, as far as happiness goes, even though I missed mother as much as any other day and even though my family was only getting worse.

***

Just as we finished singing the first song of Elder Evig's service and sat down for a minute of silence, the heavy wood door at the back of the Assembly Hall slowly opened. Whoever was entering was bent on subduing the sound of the creak it made, but it creaked anyway, tearing through the solemn silence, loudly proclaiming their late arrival.

All heads turned, craning to see who it was.

I burned with humiliation. There they were — Aunt Tala, Grandmother Min, Grandfather Daun, and ... not father. He got his way with them. He was having his peace at home alone.

I read their faces as they tip-toed through the worn wood door, which slowly creaked shut behind them. Aunt Tala looked embarrassed and defeated. Grandmother Min held her head high, smiling at her friends who sat among the gawkers. Grandfather Daun followed behind and mouthed silent apologies.

Mira's shoulders were bouncing in a fit of amusement, her tail tip stuffed in her mouth to suppress her laughter. I didn't have to suppress anything but tears. I was sad, not amused, sad for all of them, mostly for father.

Eager, no doubt, to stir the least commotion possible, my family looked for seats in the back of the Assembly Hall. Aunt Tala spotted Mira and me, and since there was room on either side of us, that was where they sat.

"Schooch down," I whispered to Mira.

Aunt Tala sat next to me.

"Your father's impossible," she whispered in my ear.

"I feel sorry for him," I whispered back.

"Why would you feel sorry for that man? He's an ingrate."

"Shhhh, be quiet," hushed a woman sitting behind us.

I leaned forward and peered down at my family's faces. They were fuming, all right. To my other side, Mira's shoulders still bounced.

Unlike father, I liked service, all the singing and the stories of struggle that two or three people volunteered to tell and Elder Evig's commentary on them, which usually made good sense to me. By the time service was over, I always felt happier in some way. Sometimes I even felt wiser. But not today. I kept thinking of father, sitting home alone, refusing help. I vowed never to be stubborn, which seemed to always hurt the stubborn one just as much as those around them, who are left to put up with the consequences.

After service, I found Elder Evig's wife.

"Madam Evig, can I talk to you privately?"

"Of course, Lin," she said, "you've been in my thoughts. Let's go to the covered courtyard, there will be no one there today."

I had to fight the temptation to tell her what happened that morning. Instead, I told her of the nightmare I had in school and how well Teacher Hana handled it.

"I've known Hana all her life," Elder Evig's wife said, "and she was very much like you when she was a child."

"Like me?"

"Older and wiser for her years. Keenly perceptive of goodness and the higher values of love."

"The higher values of love…. I don't know what that means," I said, "but I like the sound of it. It sounds like poetry."

"The values of love, Lin, are the *ways* of love — kindness, fairness, honesty, patience — and yes, they are like poetry. A life of love is like a work of art that you give to others and leave to the world."

"I want to live a life of love."

"I believe you will, Lin. But you must remember that wanting and doing are not the same. It's easy to want to live a life of love, but it's not easy to do."

"Why?"

"Because it requires effort, unlike breathing or growing taller, which happen on their own, without any thought or effort on your part. When we do as love would do, it's not an automatic happening. It's a choice we make, one among many."

"Like a poem, it doesn't write itself."

"Yes, Lin, yes," she said. Though Elder Evig's wife was old, her eyes and smile could have belonged to a woman mother's age. "There are two ways of living, Lin. Automatic living or creative living. Animals live automatically. They don't make choices like we do."

"Teacher Hana says animals have instincts instead of thoughts."

"That's right. Now, we have instincts too, but we also have the ability to think about things and make good choices and grow wise over time."

"I want to be wise."

Elder Evig's wife smiled and leaned close to me. "You *are* wise for your age," she said, "and you will grow in wisdom, I'm sure of it."

"Does being wise mean I'll live a poetic life?"

"If your purpose is love, yes."

"I guess you can't go wrong with love."

"Love is the best guide for how to live our daily life. We make many choices in a day. Some large, some small. And in every choice we make, we can stop and ask ourselves, 'what would love do?'"

"What would love do ... I like that, Madam Evig. You know a lot about love."

"I've lived a long time. And now," she said, "tell me about the nightmares you've been having."

***

"She told me that nightmares are natural after suffering a tragedy," I told Teacher Hana after school the next day. "She said mother's drowning was a great tragedy."

"It was," said Teacher Hana, "for all of us who knew her, but especially for you and your father. What else did she say?"

"That what happened was overwhelming to me, especially because I'm so young and because I was there when it happened. She asked me to tell her all the feelings I've been having. Of all of them, she said that guilt is the most damaging."

"Guilt?" Teacher Hana asked, more surprised at the word than Elder Evig's wife was. "Do you feel responsible for your mother's death?"

I nodded that I did.

"Did Mrs. Evig say anything about that?"

"She said I'm not to blame in any way."

"And do you believe that's true?"

"More than before. But she told me that guilt won't instantly go away just because I stop believing it's my fault. She said strong feelings leave a deep footprint in the sand, and it takes a while for the water to wash the footprint away. I asked her what the water is."

"What did she say?"

"Three things—love, courage, and forgiveness."

"That's quite beautiful."

"Like poetry, right?"

"Yes," Teacher Hana smiled, "like poetry. And the nightmares? Did she give you any helpful advice?"

"She said that nightmares happen when there are too many footprints that aren't being washed away. If I ignore the footprints during the day, they'll fill my dreams at night. That's how she said courage works. She said I need to be brave and face my bad feelings and talk about them with at least one person who loves me."

"I like the advice she gave you," Teacher Hana said. She sounded like mother in that moment.

"Me too. I'm glad I talked to her. I'm going to follow her advice."

And I did.

At Elder Evig's wife's suggestion, I used love and courage and forgiveness to treat my nightmares. I told Mira about my feelings at least a little every day. She always listened with patience, and I always felt better afterward. At night, when I curled up on my sleepingcushion, I forgave everything and everyone I was angry at, one by one. Then I loved everything and everyone I didn't love, even murtali waterspiders, which got less difficult with practice. I imagined that my sleepingcushion, and me in it, were floating on an ocean of love, where I was safe and life was whole, even though mother was gone and my family was going mad.

TURNING FATHER

Father bellowed, "Absolutely not!"

"But *why*, father?"

"I don't trust those people."

"I know, I know," I said, "but what does that have to do with *me*?"

"It has everything to do with you. I'm your father, and until you're grown and married, I'm your protector."

"What's there not to trust?" I asked him. "The Continentals are good people. Kind people. I think they're the best people in the world."

He shook his head. "You don't know them, Lin."

"You don't either."

"I hear stories," he said.

"Stories from who?"

"It doesn't matter."

"It *does* matter, father."

"Lin, I've told you you're not going, and that's final. And I don't want to hear another word about the Continentals and their library."

"But the stories you hear, they're all—"

"Did you not hear me?" he shouted.

"Lies," I mumbled.

Father squinted at me and shouted some more. "*Lies?!* You're a child, Lin! A *child!* You know nothing about the world! Nothing!"

He was so fuming mad, I thought I'd be injured just looking at him.

"I'm not a child," I said. "I'm ten years old."

"What's going on here?" It was the voice of Grandmother Min, who lived in the second quad of the fishing quarters. We lived in the first quad, so our two homes were as close as two homes could be. "Jorn, are you shouting at your daughter?"

"Mother, this doesn't involve you. Lin and I just finished our discussion. You can go home now."

Grandmother Min didn't go as he asked. She walked toward me, arms outstretched, and said, "Lin, how are you darling? I haven't seen you in a few days."

"Mother," father said through gritted teeth.

She looked at him with motherly disapproval. "Jorn, Lin is grieving the loss of her mother. She needs your kindness, just as you want the kindness of others, including her, I would imagine. Now I don't know what you're arguing about, but nothing under the sun warrants such angry tones. She's a young girl, not one of your teenage apprentices."

"Thank you, mother," father said, "now I kindly ask you to leave. If you want to visit with Lin, you may do so elsewhere."

"Well," she said, "seeing that Tala's away and Lin has no one else to defend her, I'm inclined to stay and help you two solve this problem."

"The problem's been solved," father told her.

"I don't believe it has," she said. "Now, which do you prefer, Jorn, that I stay and help you resolve your differences, or that Lin and I go next door, where she can tell me everything that happened here?"

"Aaahhhh, don't be impossible, mother."

"I'm not being impossible," she said, "you are. If I were being impossible, I wouldn't be giving you a choice. So which is it, shall we stay or shall we go?"

I sat silently, in awe of the entire moment. I'd never yelled at my father with such bravery. I'd never not cried when he's yelled at me the way he just did. And I'd never seen Grandmother Min treat father like a child. I was happy that she was there to stand up for me. It's what mother would have done, except without the scolding.

"Aaahhhh," was all father said as he paced around the room. From where I was sitting, I could better see his limp, how bad it really was. It was always worse when he was upset. I told mother about that once and she said that agitation can make a person's pains and ailments worse than they already are. I felt sorry for father, for his agitation and the pain he endured every day. I wanted to say something sweet and kind, but knew it might only make him angrier.

I closed my eyes and wondered what love would do and thought love would probably say those sweet and kind things. Since bickering was getting us nowhere, I decided to take a risk and go with love. I summoned some courage and said, "father, I'm really sorry you're angry, and I'm sorry you have so much pain."

He looked at me for an instant and then down again at the ground. His eyes were sad. I had more to say.

"I'm sorry you don't like the people of the Continent. But please, let Grandmother Min stay and talk about this. Please?"

"This is about the Continentals," she said.

"Yes," I told her, glad I'd mentioned it. Now it was out in the open.

Father was quiet, pacing and agitated, like the animal sentinels who pace the edges of their pens and get testy at the slightest sign of a distant storm.

"Father," I asked, "why won't you let me go to the World Library? What's the *real* reason?"

"I don't trust those people," he mumbled.

We were back to where we started, but at least I got him talking again. And Grandmother Min was here now, a real-life voice of reason who had some authority over him.

"But you don't know them," I said. I thought of the story mother told me about the man with the stick protecting the children from the grandis. Father was only seeing the man and his stick. He didn't see the children or the grandis. He didn't see the full picture.

"I don't need to know them," father said.

"But isn't that unfair to them?" Grandmother Min asked him.

"They have a motive, a hidden motive. I don't like it."

"Motive?" I asked. "What motive?"

"Answer me this," he said, "who would give the world free energy and ask for nothing in return? That doesn't smell right to me."

"What about goodness?" I said.

Father spun on his leg to face me. "*Goodness?*" he hollered.

Grandmother Min stepped between us. She was angry. "Jorn," she said, "don't you *ever* raise your voice at Lin like that."

"Mother," he said, "Lin is my daughter. Why can't you understand that I'm trying to protect her?"

"Yes, but you fail to see that Lin was protected by Lana in many ways, and sometimes from you yourself."

Father stopped his pacing and stood still as a statue.

"Fathers aren't the only protectors," she went on, "mothers protect too. And inasmuch as you are without a wife, Lin is without a mother."

Father closed his eyes and told her, "If you think Lana's death gives you license to interfere in my life and my fatherhood, then—"

Grandmother Min interrupted, "If you think that Lana's death gives you the right to be a belligerent fool, then *you* are interfering in your fatherhood."

Father started to speak, but Grandmother Min held up her hand to silence him.

"Be reasonable, Jorn." Her voice was softer now. "I don't want to bring up painful memories, but I need to in order to make my point. The loss of a wife is one of the greatest hardships a man will suffer, especially so young in life. I would say the loss of Lana is a far greater injury than the loss of your leg, and it's going to take a while to heal. Lin is suffering this injury too. You're suffering it together. Your leg injury was yours alone. But this injury is yours *and* Lin's. You can choose to let your shared suffering bring you closer to each other or pull you apart. The choice is yours." She looked at me and nodded. "The choice is yours, too, Lin."

We fell into a long silence. Father stood motionless, slightly slumped, and stared at the floor. Grandmother Min stood perfectly straight — smiling, but not kindly — and stared at father.

The silence was so heavy, I feared the words that would break it. This seemed like one of those monumental, life-changing moments when my whole future would be decided by the next few words spoken. I wondered what could I say to turn it my way, but my mind came up empty.

I closed my eyes and thought of mother. Words came easily then.

"I want to be closer, father, not pulled apart," I said. "I couldn't bear it if we let that happen."

Father turned toward me. His stone-dead eyes had life in them again, life and tenderness.

"I couldn't either," he said.

It wasn't much, but my heart leapt as if he'd just given me the world.

"I love you, father," I said, "and I'm glad we have each other."

"I love you, too, Lin. Don't let my actions make you think otherwise. I do love you."

"That's lovely, Jorn," said Grandmother Min.

I saw by the smile on father's face that even a grown man likes praise from his mother.

"I have an idea," she said, "why don't you and Lin and Tala have dinner at our house tonight? I'll make some stufferfish and asi cakes." She smiled and winked at me. I sensed she had a plan. Father's favorite food was stufferfish.

She did have a plan. After the stufferfish was served, she turned to my grandfather.

"Did you know that Lin has taken an interest in visiting the World Library at the Continent's Embassy Island? They have clarkon on display there, and she wants nothing more than to see it."

"Is that right, Lin?" he asked.

"Yes," I said, "and Aunt Tala's agreed to take me, if I get permission to go."

I looked at father to check his mood. He was busy with his fish.

"And how does one get to the Embassy Island?" Grandfather turned and asked me.

"By boat from Kuli," I said.

Grandmother Min's face lit up like a seabeacon in the night. "Oh, *Kuli*," she said. She obviously knew the place, and she obviously liked it.

"I haven't thought of Kuli in ages!" Grandfather Daun liked it too.

"You've been there?" I asked.

"I apprenticed there three seasons," he said, "It's where I met your grandmother."

"Didn't you once meet some people of the Continent there, dear?" she asked him.

"Yes," he said. "Some young folks."

I choked on my stufferfish. "You've met some Continentals?"

My grandfather smiled and nodded.

"What were they like?" I asked him.

"They were friendly and chipper and good-mannered, far more than most people you meet."

"And what were they doing in Kuli?" Aunt Tala asked.

"They were on their way to a small village to install a water purification system."

"Did you like them?" I asked my grandfather.

At the far end of the table, father cleared his throat. It sounded like a clearing of agitation, not a clearing of necessity. I looked at his face. It was expressionless.

"We all liked them," Grandfather said. "They were polite. Energetic and bright. They sure left an impression on us. We talked about them for days. They bought fish from our boat." He laughed. "They bought all of it, everything we had. And more from another fishing boat."

Father finally spoke. "What'd they do with all that fish?"

"They said they were taking it to the villagers since they so rarely get to eat it fresh."

"That was nice," I said.

"Why do you suppose these people are so nice?" father asked.

My grandfather shook his head. "Can't really say for sure."

"They believe in helping others who are less fortunate than them," said Aunt Tala.

"That's why they share their technology with other countries," I said. "Like our energy relay dish."

"There's nothing free in this world," father scoffed. "They must be up to something."

Grandmother asked him, "And what would they be up to?"

"Making those they help beholden to them."

"And what have they ever asked of us since our energy relay dish was installed?"

"Give them time, mother, give them time."

"Jorn," said Aunt Tala, "why must you distrust altruism? Just because it's not in your nature doesn't mean others aren't capable of it."

"Who would put their Embassy Islands all over the world," father said, "saying they're there to help people? You can't give that much help without getting something back. You have to wonder what they're getting out of it."

"The joy of helping," I said.

"There you go," nodded Grandmother Min.

"Aaahhhh."

I asked father, "Remember all the nice things you used to do for mother? Things she didn't even ask you to do, like making dinner on nights she had school meetings? And always asking Fisherman Clee for imports of velvetfish? And doing her chores when she didn't feel well?"

Father cracked a smile.

"Remember, Jorn," Aunt Tala said, "when you campaigned in secret to the School Board and won her promotion to Upper School?"

"I remember that," said Grandmother Min. "And I remember when we learned that Lana was allergic to hinterweed and you cut down every hinterweed bush around the house and on the paths to market and to school, everywhere she ever walked. You would have cleared all of Bree of hinterweed if you could."

"And remember how—?"

"All right," father said, "what are you all getting at?"

"Didn't it make you happy to do nice things for her?" Aunt Tala asked.

"It did," father said. "It made me happy because I loved her. She was my wife!"

"See, father?" I said. "It feels good to do good."

"Well said," said Grandmother Min. "It feels good to do good. That's been true in my life."

"But to do good for masses of people you don't even know," father said, "that's different."

"You've done good for people you didn't know," I said. "I see you picking up debris from the boat dock and the beach all the time. Especially when there are Northerners around."

"Debris is an eyesore," he said.

"Is that really why you do it?" Grandmother asked him.

"Yes, I don't want to look at debris. Bree's a beautiful village, but not when there's garbage lying about."

"Do you feel happy after you pick up the debris?" I asked.

Father didn't answer. He said instead, "Why are you persisting with me like this? Why am I the brunt of your ... whatever it is you're up to?"

"Because Lin wants to go to the World Library," said Grandmother Min, "and you're the only one standing in the way of it."

"So *that's* what this is about," father said.

"Didn't you know?"

"No, Tala, apparently I'm not clever enough to know when I'm being played by my own family."

"It's only because of your prejudice and your stubbornness," Grandmother said.

"Prejudice?"

"Prejudice," she said. "Plain and simple. You have prejudice against the people of the Continent. And you can have all the prejudice you want, Jorn, but not at the expense of my granddaughter's happiness."

Grandfather Daun spoke up. "Why don't you make it easy on everyone, Jorn, and let Lin go?"

"Yes, Jorn, let her go," Aunt Tala said.

"Do it, honey," said Grandmother Min. "Let her go."

Aunt Tala and my grandparents were on my side. That made it four against one. A tough match-up even for a man like father. I looked at him, a full-on stare, and I wasn't going to take my eyes off him until he said yes, which, by the look on his face, seemed possible. Some of his inner sanctum of sweetness shone through his eyes, which circled around the table and landed on me.

"All right," he nodded. "All right."

I was so happy I squealed, leapt from my seat, and ran to shower him with gratitude. I hugged him from behind and kissed him on the head. "Thank you, father! You've made me so happy! So, so happy! *Supremely* happy!"

"All right, Lin," father laughed. "I'm happy that you're happy."

"I love you, father."

"I love you, too, Lin."

"I promise, father, you won't regret this."

"All right," he said. "Now finish eating. And no thumping."

I stopped thumping, sat down to my stufferfish, and finished eating even though I had no hunger.

I was going to the World Library at the Continental Embassy Island. I was going to see clarkon and how the real world lived.

THE WATERTAXI TO KULI

"Four more days, girls. Four more days!" I popped a few wistberries in my mouth. "Only four more days," I sang.

Bissa groaned. "You're wearing my patience thin with all your annoying joy."

"That's not very nice," I said.

"I'm just speaking the truth," she said. "You've turned tiresome. I could be at the marketplace right now. A new picture book came in."

"Animals of the World?" Mira asked.

"No, *Volcanoes of Wershonia."*

"Well, go then," I said, "if you'd rather be there."

My feelings were hurt but I hid the fact. Bissa stood quietly for a long time, pulling clumps of wistberries from the shrubs that encircled us, staring down the slope of Mount Tantrill at the marketplace she couldn't see from here. Mira was scribbling on the pages of her kipper-paper notebook. I turned away and slipped into a daydream of riding a watertaxi to the Continental Embassy Island.

"All right," Bissa said after a while, "I'll stay. On one condition. You've got to tone it down, Lin."

"Tone what down?"

"You know, four more days and all your happiness."

"You don't want me to be happy?"

Mira giggled.

"I don't want you to be *annoyingly* happy," Bissa said. "It's a bore."

"It's just temporary," I said. "I'll stop being annoying after I get back." I held out a cluster of wistberries and smiled. "Peace offering."

Bissa took the berries. "Peace accepted."

We bumped elbows to seal the peace, and she brilliantly changed the subject.

"Still no nightmares?" she asked.

"Nope," I said. "Not one since the day father said I could go to the Embassy Island. Shows you how supreme happiness is a cure for anything."

"Maybe you'll never have nightmares again," Mira said.

"I sure hope so. Hey," I remembered to ask, "either of you ever been on a watertaxi?"

"Yep," said Mira, "a couple of times."

"Yep," said Bissa, "a bunch."

I thought about the one and only time I had ever been on a watertaxi. It was a humorous memory, and a laugh slipped out.

"You laughed," Mira said. I knew it was a question.

"I was just thinking about a watertaxi ride my family took to my Aunt Cadi's wedding," I said. "It was five years ago, and it was pretty hilarious. Want to hear it?"

"Sure," said Bissa.

"Absolutely," said Mira.

"Thirteen of us piled into the watertaxi," I said. "I remember because twelve was the limit, and the captain wouldn't take all of us. But father charmed him and talked him into letting us all go together instead of splitting into two boats, which would've made us late. I sat on the front bench. My cousin Tok was on one side and father was on the other. I'd never been on any boat but father's, which is really slow compared to a watertaxi. When it pulled away from the dock and started to speed up, cousin Tok and I went out of our minds with excitement."

"I'm flying!" I shouted. It was as if we *were* flying, low over the water like a seabird. It was a magnificent sensation, and I liked it. I loved it. The wind peeled back my face and pinned my ears down, making the whole world sound muffled. A thick mist of water sprayed up from the front of the boat, forming a light drizzle of fizzy raindrops that tickled when they fell on my face and arms. I stretched my arms out, closed my eyes, and pretended I was a seabird, gliding effortlessly over the sea.

It was the most fun I'd ever had, but sitting on a bench wasn't giving me the full flying experience I deserved. I drew my legs up under me and, taking hold of father's shoulder, stood up on the bench.

"Lin, careful!"

No sooner had he shouted the words, I was knocked back by the force of the wind. I fell right into the perfectly positioned lap of Aunt Tala.

"Ouch!" she screamed, right in my ear.

I had landed softly, without a single injury, but my ear rang for an hour after that. Aunt Tala didn't do so well, though. My head hit her chin, and hard.

"Sorry, Aunt Tala!" I looked up at her and saw the damage. Little drops of green glistened on her chin.

"I'm bleeding!" she yelled. "Lin!"

"Sorry."

"Sorry doesn't make the blood go back in!"

Mira and Bissa laughed.

"That's a great story," Mira said, "do you mind if I write it?"

"Sure," I said. "Just change the names of the innocent. It was so funny, Tok and I couldn't stop laughing. And that made Aunt Tala even more mad. But the tragically funny part came later. All day at the wedding, Aunt Tala was constantly asked, 'What happened to your chin?'"

Mira and Bissa laughed again. I half-laughed. I didn't find it as funny as I did then, probably due to the fact that I had grown to like and love Aunt Tala. Even though I'd injured her by accident, her day was ruined. She complained all the way home.

> "No one asked about *me*. 'How are *you*, Tala?' 'How is your new bookkeeping job going?' 'Are you dating anyone?' No, they only asked about my chin. Who cares about my chin? I'm an entire person, I have a life! You would expect this kind of vapid triviality to come from complete strangers, but from my own family?"
>
> "All right, Tala, we got it now," said father.
>
> "Thanks a lot, Jorn," she snipped at him. "You can't give me one little crumb of compassion? This has been the most depressing day of my life, and now my own brother takes a shot."
>
> "That wasn't a shot of anything," father said.
>
> And so it went, all the way home.

It was weeks before Aunt Tala was nice to me again. She didn't give up her grudge until father had his accident with the grangefish. None of us had any idea that day on the watertaxi that six weeks later father's life would change forever. After that, the chin incident was instantly forgotten. Aunt Tala never spoke of it again.

But I did, five years later, on the day she and I boarded a watertaxi for our grand adventure to the Continental Embassy Island.

"Remember Aunt Cadi's wedding?" I asked her.

"Aunt Cadi's wedding," Aunt Tala said, smiling with a shake of her head. "I remember." She love-tugged my ear with a playful pinch.

"I really didn't mean to hurt you," I told her.

"I know," she said. "An accident's an accident."

"But you were really mad at me for a long time."

"I was, and you know what? You deserve an apology." She love-tugged my ear, tenderly this time, and said, "I'm sorry, Lin, for blaming you. I acted immaturely."

"And that's not the person you want to be."

"No, Lin, that's not the person I want to be."

"And actually, you aren't. You've changed a lot in five years. You're more adult now. And you're more kind."

"Thank you, Lin."

In a spontaneous moment of sweetness, I reached up and love-tugged her ear. It made her laugh. Children, even older children, never love-tugged adults. It was always the other way around.

"You know," she said, "my anger really wasn't at you."

"Serious?"

"Serious. I was mad at Bau Tinli. I was hurt, really. Hurt and mad."

"Bau Tinli?"

"A fellow I knew from accounting school. We were sweet on each other, but he was shy and when we graduated from school, I didn't hear from him much. I didn't know he would be at the wedding, but there he was. Small world."

"What happened?"

"Except for mostly ignoring and avoiding me, he had one short conversation with me. The first thing he said was, 'What happened to your chin?'"

"Oh, cruel."

"It was heartbreaking," she said. "I thought I'd never get over it."

"And then father had his accident."

"Yes."

"And that changed everything."

"It changed your lives completely. Upside down and sideways." She squeezed my hand. "I don't know how you made it through."

"I don't know how we made it through, either."

"No, I mean you, how *you* made it through. I felt terribly for your father and your mother, but I felt most sorry for you."

"Why me?"

Aunt Tala looked at me with moist, kind eyes — moist not from seaspray, but from tears so small they hadn't yet fallen. "You didn't get the most adequate care and attention," she said. "Your mother was consumed with taking care of your father. He was difficult and demanding. I think taking care of him day and night drained a lot of life out of her. She was always exhausted. But it was partly her fault."

"Her fault?" I never thought of anything as being mother's fault.

"She was offered help," Aunt Tala said. "Nursing assistance. But she refused it. She insisted on taking care of him herself. Your grandparents pleaded with her to accept the nursing assistance, and your mother's mother did too."

"I didn't know any of this."

"Your mother had a stubborn streak, and it didn't always serve her well."

"How did it not serve her?"

"She liked things to be done a certain way, and they weren't always the best way."

"Like what?"

"Well, Doctor Taal gave her medicine to help with her headaches and exhaustion. She took them home and threw them away. Twice I found her bags of medicine in the dregbox."

"That's so sad."

"It is, Lin, it is sad."

"I didn't know any of this, Aunt Tala. If I knew, maybe I could have helped."

"She didn't seem to want it. She refused good help and good advice. That's what I mean when I say her stubbornness didn't serve her well."

"To tell you the truth, Aunt Tala, it's hard to hear this."

"Is this upsetting you, Lin? How did we get to talking about this anyway? This is your big day. Our thoughts and conversation should be on happier things."

"It's upsetting because I didn't know."

"You were a young child."

"Yes, but even as I got older, I didn't see mother's stubbornness."

"You saw all of her good qualities and rightly so," Aunt Tala said. "She had more good qualities than anyone I ever knew."

"I still miss her every day. When I wake up in the morning it takes a while to remember that she's not here. When I remember, it feels like she died all over again."

Aunt Tala put her arm around me and rocked me side to side for a long time. "Oh, sweetie," she said, "I so wished that had never happened. We would all be happier if she were still with us."

"I don't know why life has to be so hard, Aunt Tala. Why do so many bad, horrible things happen?"

"I'm not sure," Aunt Tala said. "For reasons we can't fathom. All I know is what Elder Evig says, we are perfection perfecting. Perfecting means you're not perfect yet."

"I don't like perfecting. I think it should all start perfect and get more perfect."

"I do, too, Lin. I do, too."

It was odd, our voyage to Kuli. I thought it would be one of the happiest boat rides of my life. It was one of the saddest. I couldn't believe that mother wasn't the person I thought she was. How could I have missed her stubbornness? I lived with her every day, but not once did I think she was being stubborn. Father was always the stubborn one, not her.

I wondered how much else about mother I didn't know.

I wondered how much about father I didn't know.

And I wondered how many things I thought were true *weren't true at all.*

If that's what adulthood is — finding out how much you don't know — it may not be as completely great as I'd thought. I was wrong about mother's stubbornness, maybe I was wrong about adulthood too.

TOUCHING CLARKON

"So you're here to see some clarkon," said the kind-eyed man as he took my hand and helped me up on the boat.

"What kind of boat is this?" I asked him.

"Well, I could call it by many names, but for you, I will say that it's a clarkon boat."

"A clarkon boat?"

"Much of this boat is made of clarkon materials."

I trembled. "I'm standing on clarkon?"

"No," he said, "you're standing on a triblock copolymer. If you want to see some of the clarkon structure, follow me." He looked over to Aunt Tala and said, "May I take you and your daughter to the boat's edge? She's expressed interest in clarkon, and she can get a good look at it there."

Aunt Tala stared silently at him as if he were from another planet and talked in a language she didn't understand. Maybe she was impressed with his big words. Maybe she was surprised that he spoke our language so well. Or maybe she was growing sweet on him. Her stare had the look of a love-trance.

I broke the awkward silence. "She's my aunt. Aunt Tala. And I'm Lin."

"It's a pleasure to meet you," the man smiled. "My name is Tyne."

"It's a pleasure to meet you too," I said. I closed my eyes and dipped my head, a spontaneous variation of a loveblink I invented just for him and this occasion. He dipped his head too, but with his eyes open. They were large and round and their black centers were encircled with a thin band of brilliant blue. No wonder Aunt Tala was sweet on him.

"That's very kind of you," Aunt Tala said. "Lin is supremely fascinated with clarkon. We'd very much like you to show us."

Supremely? Aunt Tala never said supremely. That had always been my word in the family. Tyne was definitely having an effect on her. For a moment, I felt like *I* was the older one, Aunt Lin and little Tala.

"This way, then," he said.

Tyne led us through a maze of light blue shiny chairs, arranged in small and large circular clusters. I looked down at the triblock something that we were walking on. It too was kind of shiny, but not slippery. It had a soft, clinging surface that my feet stuck to, as if I was walking on a giant piece of trusstape, the kind Aunt Tala used to stick reminder notes on our front door. Father would have loved this triblock material. Many times I'd seen him slip and curse on the deck of his boat. I wondered if the Continentals had some for sale and how much it cost. I imagined giving some to father for his birthday and how happy he would be.

"Now come over here, Lin," I heard Tyne say from a distance. He and Aunt Tala were already at the boat's edge.

I walked past a circle of blue shiny chairs where four people sat, laughing and talking in a language I didn't understand. I liked the sound of it, though, melodic and cheerful. Had I not something important to see, I would have liked to sit nearby and listen.

I found Aunt Tala and Tyne standing dangerously near the boat's edge.

"Watch out!" I yelled.

The boat had no railing, no sidewall, nothing to protect them from falling into the sea. One step and down they'd go. What kind of boat doesn't have railings?

"Watch out!" I yelled again. "You're about to fall in!"

They only laughed at me.

"We're in no danger, Lin," Tyne said. "This is clarkon."

He passed his hand in the empty space where should have been, but wasn't, a rail. His hand stopped short and made a thud.

"It's invisible," Aunt Tala said.

"What?"

"See for yourself."

I reached into the empty space and there it was. Clarkon. I was touching clarkon! I closed my eyes and ran my hand along its smooth surface. "Does the entire boat have a sidewall of clarkon?"

"It does, "said Tyne. "And as you might guess, it serves a dual purpose. It provides safety, and it offers a view of the water's surface. The volo fish always swim near the boat when it's moving. They give a marvelous show."

I had heard of volo fish, who leap into the air to snatch the insects they feed on.

"I've never seen a volo fish."

"Nor have I," Aunt Tala said.

Tyne smiled. "You will today. And you will see even greater things."

"They say clarkon is stronger than anything in the world," I told him.

"It is indeed," he smiled. "Tell me, isn't the grandis the largest animal in Wershonia?"

"Yes," I nodded.

"All right, hold an image of a grandis in your mind, then pinch this clarkon sidewall and feel how thick it is."

I pinched the sidewall. "As thin as a small raindrop," I said.

"That's about right," Tyne said. "Now imagine we turn this piece of clarkon on its side and try to pierce it with a sharp, pointed knife. It would require the weight of *ten* grandises, maybe more, to pierce through."

"Ten grandises," Aunt Tala said as she hit the sidewall with her fist.

I imagined ten grandises, each standing on the broad, bowled back of the grandis below him. The grandis on the bottom was balancing with one foot on the end of the knife handle, which I made fat and flat to help him out. This stack of grandises stretched high into the sky. "That seems impossible to me," I said.

"It's due to the remarkably strong bond between the carbon atoms," Tyne told me, "which is what clarkon is — carbon atoms, very tightly bound. Mothing more, nothing less."

"Carbon," I said, "a basic building block of life."

While Tyne praised my knowledge of science, a high-pitched siren sang three notes. It was a beautiful sound, not ugly and alarming like the storm siren at home, meant to scare you into seeking protection.

"What's that?" I asked.

"That signal means we depart in ten minutes," Tyne said. "And while we've been talking, a majority of our passengers have arrived. More are still to come. It's a full boat today. And it's time, unfortunately, for me to return to my work."

"What exactly do you do?" Aunt Tala asked.

"I orient the first-time passengers, and I'm one of fifteen interpreters. I speak both of the Wershonian languages and Egli as well."

Egli? "You let Eglians visit the Embassy Island?"

"We welcome everyone one who wants to visit."

"That's very gracious," I said. "Don't you think, Aunt Tala?"

"I do, yes. Now let's let Tyne do his work, Lin." She turned to him and said, "Thank you for taking the time to speak with us."

"It was my pleasure." He smiled and dipped his head then disappeared in the thickening crowd.

The boat was awash in an ocean of ears, some tall and slender, some short and stubby, some painted pretty, and some bent forward like Mira's. I couldn't wait to tell her.

"Let's walk around and see the different people," I said to Aunt Tala.

Her eyes grew large and a wide grin came over her. "Yes," she said, "let's."

The people's voices blended in a garbled but pretty symphony of life. This was the first time I'd ever seen so many people from different places in one place at one time. I wondered if any of them were Eglian. I led our way through the crowd, my heart beating fast with excitement and wonder. I felt we had entered a place where the whole world existed.

Ahead was a man and a woman and a girl about my age. They had the yellow-green eyes of Southern Wershonians, but they weren't speaking. They looked worried.

"Do you think they're having trouble, Aunt Tala?"

"Well, it's really not our business," she said.

"But if they need help, shouldn't we help them?"

"There are those like Tyne whose job it is to help them. We're here to visit the Library. Don't create trouble by trying to help where it's not needed."

The girl looked the most worried. I felt sad for her and decided to turn toward them so that we could walk closely by.

"This way, Aunt Tala, I want to see something over there." I pointed at nothing in the distance, and Aunt Tala followed me.

I walked toward the family, ready to smile at any of them who looked at me. When I was about to pass the girl, I said in a loud voice, my eyes on the girl, "Right over there, Aunt Tala!"

I'd gotten her attention. She looked right at me.

"Hello," I said.

"Hello," she said. She spoke Welbi too. "Where are you from?"

"Bree," I told her. "In Strellin."

"I'm from Donnot in Tobbs."

"Then that makes us neighbors."

"You're right," she smiled, "national neighbors."

"I'm Lin," I said.

"I'm Vola."

"Are you here to see the World Library?"

"No, we're here because I'm applying to the International Schools. I have two interviews with the admissions counselors."

"International Schools?"

"Yes, you don't know about them?"

"No."

"Here they are!" a man cried behind me. It was Vola's father. He said to her mother, "I'll be back, darling." Then he kissed the top of Vola's head and whispered in her ear, "Don't worry, sweetheart, it's all going to work out."

"Sounds like you escaped a close call," I said to Vola.

"Super close," she said. "My school couldn't find my paperwork, and you can't apply without it. The school secretary collected my grades from all my past teachers. We weren't sure if she'd be here with them before the boat left."

"Tell me about these schools," I said. I could hear Vola's mother telling Aunt Tala about them, but I wanted to hear it directly from Vola. That would give Aunt Tala and I double the information.

"There are three of them," Vola said, "each one on an island of the Continent."

"The Continent? That's where these schools are?"

"Yes, but not on the mainland, on the islands. Students can't travel to the mainland for two years."

"How long are you at these schools?"

"From thirteen to nineteen."

"Six years? And you live there, away from home?"

"Yes," she said. "Sounds exciting, doesn't it?"

"Supremely exciting. Though I guess you'd miss your family."

"I'm sure I will, but I'll talk to them by holophone."

"Your family has a holophone?"

"Both my parents have one," she said, "and I'm getting my own next month for my birthday. When you talk to someone on a holophone, it's like being with them in person. You can be where they are, or they can be where you are."

"Be together as you talk? How is that possible?"

"I'm not sure, but it is. You don't know about holophones?"

"Not really," I said, "we don't have any in Bree."

70

Vola's father emerged from the crowd. He was holding her paperwork high in the air.

"I've got them!" he said to Vola. "We're going to get you in, darling, we're going to get you in!"

"Now don't fill her with fat hope," Vola's mother said. "Nothing's been decided yet."

She was clearly the practical parent and he the dreamer. *It's good to have both*, I thought.

"You're a lucky girl," I said to Vola.

"Thanks, Lin. Big luck was on my side today."

A siren sang, followed by a snap and a whoosh and the whirring sound of an engine. Then came a thunk and a long hiss and an acceleration experience I would never forget. What made it spectacular was not the speed, but the lift. The hiss had raised the boat almost completely out of the water.

"Is it my imagination," I asked Aunt Tala, "or are we being lifted to the sky?"

"We're being lifted! Isn't it an odd feeling?"

"Odd and amazing!"

"Oddly amazing," Vola agreed. "Just wait, it gets better."

And it did. Three man-sized turbines began to spin, lifting us a little higher and propelling us forward, smooth and light, as if we were floating in air, which I soon learned we actually were. Our cruising speed was four times faster than a watertaxi and more than ten times faster than father's boat, which I regretted telling him later.

The sky was surly that day, and when rain broke out halfway to the Embassy Island, the boat's clarkon roof protected us in the loveliest way. We stood underneath and watched plump, heavy raindrops splat upon its invisibleness, stream down its sides, and spill into the sea.

"We're in the rain but completely dry!" I shouted, out of my mind happy.

Vola's father said something about how he was experiencing the delights of a clarkon roof as if for the first time.

"Thank you," he told me, even though I'd done nothing. He laughed and laughed at my enjoyment, laughing more than Vola and almost as much as me.

"Laugher comes easily to father," she later said.

"You're a lucky girl," I told her, stinging from a sharp bite of jealousy. "Supremely lucky."

Then I brushed away my envy as best I could. This was my day of joy.

"Wait 'til you see the Island," Vola said. "It was built by the Continentals."

"How do you build an island?" I asked.

"As I understand it," her father said, "they build the island on land and float it out to the ocean location."

"And how does it stay there?" I asked.

"They secure it to the ocean floor with clarkon ribbon."

Clarkon ribbon. I smiled.

"You're going to *love* the Embassy Island," Vola told me. "It has three big buildings that are partially invisible. Then there are smaller buildings and flowered walkways. And it's all covered by clarkon canopies in different colors. They use a lot of color on the island, not just to make it pretty, but to help people know where to go."

"How do they do that?" I asked. "Colored signs?"

"Yes, and colored arrows on the walkways that point to the different buildings. Each of the buildings is a color. The Library is blue, so if you want to find the Library from anywhere on the Island, all you have to do is follow the blue arrows."

"That's clever," I said. "I guess color's a universal language."

Vola smiled a toothy smile. "You're right, Lin," she said. "Speaking of language, have you heard they might do away with Welbi?"

"What? Who is 'they', and what do they have against Welbi?"

"The Co-National Assembly wants all of Wershonia to speak one language, and it's going to be Culti," she said.

"But why?"

"Tobbs and Strellin are the only two countries that speak Welbi," her father said. "Every one else speaks Culti."

"But I don't know Culti," I said.

Vola looked at me, her eyes wide. "You don't—?"

"No."

"At all?"

"No, no one in Bree does."

"Your schools don't teach it?" she asked.

"No. Not Nature School, not Lower School, not Upper School." Vola stared at me in disbelief. "Why," I asked, "do your schools teach it?"

She nodded. "They make us learn it, even though we don't speak it much."

"You know Culti?"

"Some."

For no good reason, I felt ashamed. "I don't know what to think about that," I said. "I like change, but I don't want to learn a whole new language."

"You needn't worry, Lin," her father said. "The younger you are, the easier it is. Vola's been tutoring me."

I imagined my father trying to learn Culti. *Impossible.* Yet more impossible was the idea that he would let me teach him anything. That would never happen. And what a relief, I wouldn't want the job. He was stubborn and a know-it-all. A know-it-all who didn't know most of what he thought he knew.

"Look," Vola said, pointing to the sky. "A sub-orbital."

I looked up, and there it was. I hollered the news to Aunt Tala, even though she'd seen them before. "Nice," I heard her say.

Vola and I sat in some squishy, pivot-seat chairs that molded to our backs and behinds and let us stretch back and face the sky. We laughed at the squishiness as we watched the sub-orbital rise high above us, silent and graceful.

"They go almost as high as the satellites," Vola said.

"Way past the clouds," I agreed. "You can see the sun up there."

"And the black of space if you go high enough."

"I read that sub-orbitals are made of clarkon."

"Yep, the Continentals love clarkon."

"*I* love clarkon," I said.

Vola chuckled. "That makes you more like a Continental than a Breean."

"Maybe so," I said, happy at the thought of it.

The sub-orbital airbus entered the cloud layer and disappeared. I smiled at the sight. It looked like the clouds swallowed the airbus for an afternoon snack.

"I love clarkon too," Vola said. "How can you not love something that does so many great things?"

I had already liked Vola, but hearing her say she loved clarkon made her a supremely appealing person. I wanted to be friends beyond today and wondered how to make that happen and if she'd want to be my friend too, even though I was two years younger.

"Tell me more about the International Schools," I asked her.

"Sure," she said. "I've read all the literature. The schools are for students who weren't born on the Continent."

"Even Eglians?"

"Sure," she said. "But you have to be smart and mature for your age. And you have to be — I like how they say it — forward-thinking and service-minded."

"Forward-thinking and service-minded. Sounds like poetry," I said.

"Then you're definitely both. And you know what that means, Lin."

"What?"

"You're an ideal applicant."

All the way to the Island, Vola and I talked about the International Schools. Aunt Tala talked with Vola's parents about them and other things too, including bookkeeping. Vola's mother was a bookkeeper in Donnot, and she and Aunt Tala both went to the same accounting school, missing each other by only four years. Small world.

A small world and getting smaller.

The Happiest Day

"All right, ladies, looks like it's just the two of you. Careful as you step. You can sit anywhere, I suppose."

"You're not the same man," I said.

"As who?"

"As this morning."

"Aw, whoever that was," he said, "his shift was over long ago. I run the night taxis."

He was a scruffy man, our watertaxi captain, rough and mangy and short on manners. Nothing at all like the Continentals I'd watched and admired all day.

It was night now, long past sunset. The cloud-to-cloud lightning was so active that the dark of night was illumined by rhythmic flashes of white and pink, which lit up the clouds as if an afternoon sun still hung in the sky.

Though the day had been long, we were exhilarated and happy.

"Aunt Tala, you're sitting in front," I said when she sat next to me on the watertaxi. "You never sit in front."

"And you *always* sit in front," she said. "I want to be next to you, so here I am."

"You'll see," I said, "it's the best place to be to feel the air and the speed, even though it probably won't seem so fast now after being on the airboat and the space elevator."

She leaned close. "I think that was my most favorite part of the day, the simulated space elevator. Traveling through the clouds, seeing the stars and the black of space, looking down at the cloudtops and our world. It seems so small from up there."

"I had lots of favorite parts today," I said. "But none were better than seeing space. Even though it was pretend, I loved it. It seemed so real, I got queasy. You know, in a good way."

"Good queasy," she nodded.

The captain pulled the watertaxi out from the dock and pointed it Breeward. We were on our way home.

The watertaxi accelerated slowly, then quickly, with the very same velocity it always had, and I was right, it was nothing to thump your tail about. It seemed to move no faster than father's boat.

When we reached cruising speed, I said to Aunt Tala, "I've never felt smarter than I do today. I learned so much so fast, I could feel my brain growing inside my head. All day long."

"Do you have any idea how bright you are for your age?"

"But didn't you feel that too? All the new things we saw and learned about, didn't each next one make your brain feel bigger?"

Aunt Tala smiled at the clouds. "My mind *does* feel bigger," she said, "and I'm most definitely smarter than I've ever been. My knowledge of science and history has increased tremendously ... in a single day."

A bright flash of lightning made the whole sky white.

"I feel like I'm not the person I used to be," I said. "There's more of me now."

"Yes," Aunt Tala said. "There's more of me too."

"I want to learn more about everything. I want to see the world and space and how people live."

Aunt Tala kissed the top of my head. "I hope you do see the world, Lin." She shook her head, smiling. "To be honest, I'm stunned at your intelligence. I'm at a loss to explain it, given your father's stock."

"There's mother's stock too."

"Yes, she was bright. Not as bright as you, though. I hope your curiosity and intelligence aren't wasted."

"What did you think about the International Schools?"

"I'm intrigued," Aunt Tala said. "You want to go, don't you?"

"Do you think I should?"

"You should answer my question first, before I tell you what I think."

"Yes," I said, "I want to go. After what I've seen today, it'll be really hard to be happy at school in Bree. Really hard."

"I'm sad to hear you say that," Aunt Tala said, "yet I completely understand."

"But it's six years away from home, and father would have to agree. Do you think he'd ever let me go?"

"I honestly don't know. Would he *want you to go?* No. Would he, in the end, *let you go?* Maybe. If you really want it, it's a fight worth fighting. Remember how adamantly opposed he was to you coming to the Embassy Island today. So, don't discount your ability to persuade him and his ability to be persuaded."

"Do *you* think I should go?"

"If you want to, yes. Absolutely yes. I think it would give you life experiences you deeply crave and opportunities that Bree could never give you. I would miss you terribly, but I know it would be good for you."

"We could talk on holophones," I said. "If we had them. Then we wouldn't miss each other. I would call every day, and we would see each other while we talk. Make faces and laugh. You could show me what you're cooking, and I could give you cooking advice. You could put father's holophone on him while he's sleeping and then I would call to wake him up." Aunt Tala laughed at the idea. "Then I would say, 'Wake up, father! It's me, Lin, on the other side of the world, here to welcome you to your day!' And he would see me and smile and then I would say to him, 'And remind you that I love you with all my heart, even though I'm far, far away.'"

"Yes, Lin, you would make it fun and that would help us miss you less. But since we don't have holophones, we would have to visit you there, which I'd have no complaints about."

"But father would," I said. "He'd never go to the Continent, not even to their islands."

Aunt Tala squeezed my hand. "I'm so sorry, Lin."

"But maybe you're right. Maybe I could convince father. What did Vola's mother tell you about the schools?"

"I asked about the cost. She said she thinks your schooling would be free since Bree's in an impoverished region."

"It costs money to go there?"

"For all but the most impoverished," she said. "And the airbus travel would be free, for you as a student and for us, if your father and I came to visit you." She read the surprise on my face. "The energy used to power an airbus is free."

"Oh, right," I said, "siphoned right off the clouds."

"No, that's for drones and smaller aircraft. To lift a sub-orbital airbus requires hydrogen, remember? A lot of it. But they have more than they need, and that's why they can fly us at no expense."

"See, Aunt Tala, you're bright too."

"I have a good memory," she said. "There's a difference."

"What else did Vola's mother tell you about the schools?"

"Students come from all over the world."

"Even Egli," I said. "Vola told me."

"Even Egli?"

"Yes, if they qualify."

"Right, of course. Now the application process is pretty involved. They want your school records, a written essay about your life and interests, letters of recommendation from five adults, three of them teachers, and then interviews with you, with your parents, and with the three of you together. That's three separate interviews."

"Maybe you could fill in for mother," I said.

"We'll have to ask about that."

"She'd be so happy for me if I went. I already told her about it."

"Your mother?"

"Yes, just a little because there was so much going on today."

"You had a conversation with your mother?"

"Yes."

"How?"

"In my mind."

"Did she answer back?"

"Not in words," I said, "but I feel her feelings, and sometimes I say words for her."

"Out loud?"

"No, silently, in my mind."

"How long have you been doing this?"

"Since about two weeks after she died. It was Elder Evig's wife's idea. She told me that her love and goodness will always be alive in my heart and that if I miss her, I can find her there."

"I had no idea," Aunt Tala said in a voice as soft as mother's.

"I've thought about telling father about it," I said, "but I'm afraid to. I don't know why."

Aunt Tala put her arm around me and gently squeezed my shoulders. "I think Mrs. Evig gave you very good advice," she said.

"I still feel sad every morning when I wake up and remember that mother's gone. But when I find her in my heart and talk to her, it's true what Elder Evig's wife said, I feel mother's love and goodness."

"If she could see what you're making of your life, she would be very proud."

"She makes me want to be a better person," I said. "I dreamt one night that I saw her after I died, and even though I was an old woman, I was so excited to tell her all about my life. But she said to me, 'I already know. I know every detail.' So, ever since that dream, I imagine that she sees and knows everything I do. And I want to make her proud of me."

"I need a tissuecloth, Lin. You've got me crying."

I turned to the boat captain, "Do you have a tissuecloth?!" I had to yell over the noise, but I was polite about it.

He shouted back, "Don't have a tissuecloth, but I have a raintowel! It's clean!"

"All right! Thanks!"

He tossed me his raintowel, and I gave it to Aunt Tala.

"You cry a lot more than you used to, you know."

"Yes," she said, "cry and shout. Your father drives me mad sometimes."

"But aside from all the yelling, you're also a lot kinder now. Kinder and sweeter and more loving and affectionate. You've really changed."

Aunt Tala put the raintowel in her lap. "I feel changed since this morning."

"Me too," I said. "Forever changed, maybe."

"Maybe."

"How do you think today has changed you?" I asked.

Aunt Tala squinted and tipped her head upward. Her face was completely relaxed, not tense and crinkled. She was smiling and beautiful, peaceful and soft. I hoped she would always be this way.

"I feel happy," she said, "because I'm filled with hope. I'm astonished at what we're capable of. Not just the satellite technology and medical knowledge and the space elevators, but the kindness and cooperation and generosity that's in us. Our ancestors, you know, were not kind and generous. They fought each other over every little thing. And in some places in the world, they still do. But all of that is to be outgrown, and you really see it in the Continentals. I think I understand better the purpose of their embassies. I think they want to show the world the goodness and compassionate kindness we're capable of showing one another. You see it in their upliftment projects."

"I want to be like that," I said. "I want to be an inspiration to other people and to make their lives better."

"I believe you will be."

"And I want to ride a real space elevator some day."

"If you travel to the Continent, I'm sure you will."

A warm joy spilled inside me. "Thank you, Aunt Tala, for bringing me here today."

She love-tugged my ear and before letting go, she whispered in it, "And thank *you* for inviting me."

Her whisper tickled my ear and made me laugh.

"This has been the happiest day of my life," I said.

Aunt Tala agreed. "It's been my happiest day too."

"And maybe I *will* travel to the Continent. Maybe like Vola, I'll go to the International Schools."

"We'll see what your father has to say."

Yes, we would see what father had to say.

MOSTLY MORE MATURE

Father pounded his fist on the table.

"If you two are going to persist in talking about the Continentals and their man-made gift-to-the-world island, then at least give me another twig of kono root!"

Aunt Tala had been hiding father's bags of kono root and making him ask for it and only then would she dole out a little. "You're having too much," she told him. "Too much. And if you can't slow it down, then I'll have to see to it that you do."

"One twig, Tala. One twig."

Aunt Tala looked at me and I at her. If it were up to me, I'd give him the twig.

"How many have you had today, Jorn?" she asked.

"You tell me, you're the dispenser."

"I'm concerned for you, don't you understand?"

"And I'm grieving the death of my wife! Don't you understand that? Have you no compassion for your brother who's taken you in?"

"Taken me in? I'm here to cook for you!"

"You prefer then to live with father and mother?"

"I prefer to be here, where I can help you and Lin. You need help, Jorn! You need help!"

This was not the worst yelling match I'd ever heard between them, but it was escalating dangerously and we were still eating dinner and, mostly, I wanted father not to hate the Continentals any more than he already did because Aunt Tala wouldn't give him a little twig of kono.

"I have something to say," I said in my most calm, mature voice. They fell silent and looked at me, Aunt Tala with interest and father with surprise.

Father cleared his throat. "And what have you to say, Lin?"

"I think you should have a twig of kono root. I think during this time of grieving, it's all right to have a little more kono than usual, but only then. When you feel better, less kono." I looked at Aunt Tala. "So don't deprive him now. Think about it. I have supreme excitement about our trip to help me with my grieving. Father only has kono root. If he had something better to help him feel happy, then I'd agree with you, but he doesn't."

***

"How'd that go over with your Aunt Tala?" Mira asked when I told her the story two days later, lying under the shiny silver energy relay dish on Mount Tantrill. Mira and I had spent every afternoon there since I got back from the Embassy Island four days earlier. It was the perfect place to tell my stories of technology and space and the Continental people and clarkon. She listened intently, asked intelligent questions, and scribbled pages of notes. Mira never tired of my endless stories.

But Bissa did. She joined us the first three days, but today went to the marketplace instead. A new shipment of flasan raincapes had just come in. Since today it was just Mira and I, I confided in her the latest madness from home.

"Aunt Tala was peeved," I said. "But only for a day."

"That's progress."

"Big progress. She's been mostly more mature since we've come back. But still, I think she was insulted that father liked my opinion more than hers. She said to him, 'You're perfectly happy to accept wisdom from a child when it suits your wishes.'"

Mira tapped her pen against her chin and smiled an impish grin. "Maybe she was jealous."

"Jealous?"

"Jealous about your fairness and compassion. Those are qualities that she lacks and that come natural for you."

"Think so?"

"Don't I know you better than anyone?"

"Yes," I said, "but Aunt Tala *is* changing. As I said, she got over her upset in a day. She doesn't hold grudges as long as she used to. It's good. She's maturing, just like we are."

"Well, I hope it sticks."

"What do you mean?"

"Sometimes people improve but it doesn't stick. Sooner or later, they go back to their old ways."

"I hope her maturity sticks like trusstape," I said. "Father eventually might like it so much that he'll start maturing too. I wonder why they don't teach maturity in school."

"Father says that'll never happen. Not in Bree."

"Really? Why?"

"A while back, Elder Evig's wife proposed to the School Committee that they teach a class on maturity. She offered to supply written teaching materials and to train a few teachers."

"What happened?"

"They couldn't agree on it," Mira said. "Father was in favor of the idea and a some of the others on the voting committee. But most of the voters said classes on maturity don't belong in the school. They say it should be the responsibility of the parents to teach maturity to their children."

"But what about kids whose parents aren't mature?" I asked.

"Really."

"When did all this happen?"

"Last year," Mira said. "I told father I wanted to write a story about it, and he said I shouldn't. Too controversial."

"That's so tragic. I think classes on maturity would do everyone good. Even kids who have mature parents and don't need the classes. They could be examples to the other kids. They probably teach maturity on the Continent, and even in the International Schools."

"Have you asked your father yet about applying?" Mira asked.

"No."

"Afraid to?"

"A little, but mostly it's too early. I have to wait for the right time. When he's in a constant tiff because Aunt Tala's hiding kono root from him, it's the absolute worst time."

Mira agreed. "I would wait." She rolled over onto her belly. "You never finished your story."

"About the kono incident at dinner?"

"No, about the space elevator."

"They make rope out of clarkon," I said, "really long rope and stronger than anything. They stretch it from the ground to the satellites. Each satellite has two elevators that move up and down the clarkon rope."

"That's convenient."

"The satellites are always exactly above the same spot on the ground. And get this, the part of the clarkon rope that's above the clouds takes energy directly from the sun and uses it to move the elevators."

"And the rope never breaks?"

"It's clarkon! Hundreds of times stronger than porvalens, and a lot lighter. Amazing, don't you think?"

Mira nodded as she scribbled in her kipper-paper notebook, humming and happy. "You know," she said when she was done, "you're the Bree expert on clarkon."

"Probably so." I laughed. "You would have liked going up the space elevator. You go into a small room the actual size and shape of a real elevator. It has a clear clarkon window all along the front and sides. You can see everything."

"All the way up?"

"All the way. I'll never forget seeing everything on the ground get smaller and smaller. Then you go into the clouds and everything's white and pink for a while. You go all the way through the clouds and out the other side, and if it's daytime, you see pure sky and pure sunshine."

"You can see the whole sun?"

"Yes, but you can't look at it. They gave us all a pair of dark sunshades because the sun would burn our eyes."

"I can't believe you saw the sun."

"It was fake sun," I said. "But now I know what it looks like. So after a while, you leave the pink sky and you're in black space, where the satellites live."

"You're right, I *would* like to see that," Mira said.

"I think every kid in Bree should go to the Embassy Island. It could be a school trip. What do you think your father would say?"

"I don't know, but it's worth asking."

"If our teachers really want to educate us, they should take us to the World Library. We know nothing about the world, Mira. Nothing."

"And don't even know it."

"Don't even know it," I agreed.

"Tell me something else you saw," Mira said.

"There are these force fields cloaks that the Continentals wear when they're in dangerous places like Egli where they do service projects. They're like invisible raincapes, but they have a really strong force field that will push away any kind of weapon so whoever's wearing it can't be hurt."

"Why would the Eglians want to hurt the Continentals if they're there to help them?"

"That's what I asked. The Eglians aren't the problem, the mine owners are. They don't want the Continentals to help the Eglian people, even though all they're doing is building better homes and teaching them how to clean their water and food. They rescue escaped slaves and find them families to live with. That's why the mine owners hate the Continentals. They're totally against slavery."

"Why is there so much meanness in people?"

"I don't know, Mira. It doesn't make sense to me. Maybe they don't know that it feels better to be kind. Someone at the Embassy Island said that if you're hurting, the best thing you can do is help someone else who's hurting more than you."

"That's brilliant," Mira said as she wrote the words.

"I'm glad I can tell you these things, Mira. I'm glad you understand."

"I wouldn't know any of this unless you told me. No one else in Bree seems to care."

"Some more than don't care," I said. "My father despises the Continentals."

"How could you not like the Continentals?"

"Right, how could you not? They're the smartest and nicest people in the world. They say that the purpose of their Embassies is to help people who want to be helped and to show how love and kindness can make everyone's life better."

Mira laughed and said what only a great writer would say. "You not only came back with great stories, Lin, you came back with inspiration."

"You're right, Mira. I went to the Embassy Island to see clarkon and came home with so much more. What a surprise."

"Life's one surprise after another, don't you think?"

I nodded. "One amazing surprise after another."

LETTERS TO VOLA

"Which is less expensive, the carrier birds or the runners?"

The toothless old man behind the counter coughed a couple times, squinted at me, and shifted a wad of something from one side of his mouth to the other. It could have been kono root, but more likely it was an asi bag — a small bag of soaked asi seeds that toothless people gnaw on for nourishment.

"That'll depend on what you're sending and where it's going," he said in a voice friendlier than his face. "We also have the carrier fish if you're sending a letter or small parcel to another coastal city."

"I'm sending a letter to the town of Donnot in the country of Tobbs," I told him.

"Just a letter, eh?"

"Yes, sir."

"And you have it with you, addressed and such?"

"Yes," I nodded.

"Carrier bird will be your best method of transport. Costs less than the runners and will get it there sooner."

"How much to send this letter?" I put my kipper-paper envelope on the counter.

He picked up my envelope and took a long, curious look at it. "Made this yourself?"

"I did. I made it in Nature School."

"My great-grandson's in Nature School. I saw the kipper-paper he made. Wasn't as nice as this."

"What's his name," I asked, "your great-grandson?"

"Jabe."

"di Groot?"

"You know Jabe?"

"Yes," I said, "we're ... friendly acquaintances."

"He's a handful, that boy."

"I think most kids our age are handfuls for our families."

"Even a nice girl like you?"

"I give my father his fair share of parental grief."

Great-grandfather di Groot and I laughed together, but I had to look away, so odd and unsightly was his toothless mouth.

"And your name is Lin di Ana," he read from my envelope.

"Yes, I'm pleased to meet you."

He put my letter on a rusty scale, squinted at his chart of numbers, and said, "That'll cost three pargens."

"Oh, that's not very much."

"Have you never sent a letter before?"

"No," I said, "this is the first time. I hoped I'd have enough money." I poured my bag of coins into my hand. One argen, two demi-argens, and six pargens spilled out. I gave him three of the pargens. "How long will it take to get to Donnot?"

"About two day's time," he said.

"That's not long at all!"

"I reckon not."

Great-grandfather di Groot and I laughed again, but this time I didn't turn away. I wondered if it had hurt to lose all those teeth.

***

"Three pargens, can you believe it?" I told Aunt Tala that night as we were cooking dinner. "I guess it costs the same to send a letter from Donnot to Bree. Isn't it amazing that I got a letter from Vola—"

"Lin! Would you pay attention!"

"Sorry."

"Sorry doesn't make the flour go back in the bowl."

"I'll clean it up."

"Thank you. And let's make a rule. No talking while cooking."

"No talking whatsoever?"

"Right."

"But what if you need to tell me something, like 'Lin, I need some turo eggs'?"

"Don't get wise with me. You know my meaning. We can talk the essentials, but nothing else."

"That doesn't seem very friendly."

"Lin, the rule is in effect now."

We silently finished making dinner, except for a few essential words, and I hated it.

"I've been thinking of going to the Nadri night Community Dance," she announced at dinner.

"That's a really good idea," I said. "That's where the single men go to look for wives."

"I'm not looking for a husband," Aunt Tala said. "I'm looking for some joy in my life. I used to love dancing when I was in Bookkeeping School. Don't know why I stopped for so long."

"I'm glad you're going to go, Aunt Tala. We should try to have joy every day. Even you, father. Maybe you should go to the dances too."

"Never."

"You can just sit and watch," I said.

"I have better things to do with my time," he grumbled.

"Wallow in your sorrows home alone?" Aunt Tala asked unkindly.

Though they were hurled at father, not me, her harsh words stung. I expected father to sling some meanness back at Aunt Tala, which some would say she deserved. But father wasn't interested in fighting. He even said so.

"This is a good dinner," he told her, "and I want to enjoy it in peace. I'm not interested in having a fight with you, Tala. Let's just end that conversation."

"Fine," she said.

"And Lin?"

"Yes father?"

"No thumping."

***

"Remember, Mira, how you said a person can change for the better, and that sometimes it sticks and sometimes it doesn't?"

"Yes," she said with a mouthful of hard-won wistberries. We dared make the muddiest hike of the year up to the wistberry groves and were elated to find a fresh crop of perfectly ripe berries, fat and sweet from two days of warm rain. "Who'd you have in mind?" she asked.

"Aunt Tala," I said. "She slipped last night."

"A fall from grace?"

"Is that what that means?"

"Yes, when you grow and mature and then you lose it."

"She lost it, all right. All the maturity she came home with after our trip to the Embassy Island — it's gone now. I thought she would *stay* mature and more adult, and she did for about a week, but last night when we were cooking, she was back to her old self."

"And you were surprised?"

"Yes," I said, "I guess I was. And disappointed. And ... confused. Is she going to stay like this?"

"Maybe not completely," Mira said. "She'll probably just be moody about it. You know, good days and bad days."

"Mature days and immature days."

"Right. It happens all the time. Believe me," Mira said, "I study people. I see it. One thing you can count on, people are never consistent and will constantly surprise you."

"Like father," I said. "He was actually nice at dinner last night. She was ready to have a fight, and he wasn't interested. Hey, that reminds me of my good news."

"Good news?"

"Despite all the moodiness at dinner last night, father said I could have dinner at Teacher Hana's every week."

"Dinner with her family?"

"Yes," I said. "Every Nadri night. It was Teacher Hana's idea."

"Why you?"

I told Mira the whole story:

"Teacher Hana," I'd said after all my schoolmates dispersed, "I've been wanting to ask you something."

"Wonderful, Lin. Let's walk and talk. I have some questions for you too."

Teacher Hana and I walked along the shoreline, away from the piers since the fishermen were arriving with their catches and making their usual commotion. Father still fished every day but Adri, so he would have been among them.

"The whole school is abuzz with your stories of the Embassy," Teacher Hana said. "I'm glad it was such a rich experience."

"I think I'll be telling stories about it for years," I said. "I was afraid I would forget some of it, but since I tell the stories over and over again, it's all staying fresh in my memory."

"My children are eager to hear your stories. They're not satisfied with the bits and pieces I tell them from what little I've overheard. And for that matter, I would like to hear more myself."

"I'd be glad to tell you sometime," I said.

"Now, you wanted to ask me something," Teacher Hana said as we walked in the wet sand under a light drizzle of rain.

"It's about the incident with Jabe di Groot."

"Yes," she said, "I remember."

"I can't stop wondering what you did that changed him.

Right before my eyes, you turned him into a nice person. The nicest I'd ever seen him. It was like you had a special power."

"Special power," she said, nodding her head and thinking before she answered. "The power you speak of isn't any power *I* have, Lin, it's love's power, and it's not so much a power as an attitude."

"What kind of attitude?"

"It's an attitude of sympathy," she said. "Of respect. Of wanting the best outcome for everyone involved. When your attitude is motivated by love, the seemingly impossible can happen. Not always, but it can."

"With love and respect you can get people to do what you want?"

"Getting someone to do what we want is not the point. I wasn't trying to change Jabe."

"But he *did* change," I said. "You made him a better person, at least for a while."

"That was Jabe's doing, note mine," she said. "He responded positively to the love and respect with which I treated him."

"So whenever you treat someone with love and respect, they'll become nicer?"

"No, not necessarily. Not everyone responds well to love."

"But Jabe did, the meanest boy in school."

"Yes, he did."

"You got through to his inner sanctum of sweetness."

"His inner sanctum of sweetness," she said. "Is that your phrase?"

"I guess I invented it. I believe that everyone, even the meanest person, has an inner sanctum of sweetness."

"So do I, Lin. That's a lovely way of thinking about it."

"Some people, like you," I told her, "don't hide their

sweetness. But some, like Jabe and my father, it's buried under their meanness."

"Yes, some people *do* have a tendency to bury their best qualities. They're rich with love and goodness and sweetness, as you say, and scarcely know it."

"My father used to be sweet, before he lost his leg."

"Yes, I knew your father then. He adored your mother and was so good to her."

"What was your impression of my father back then?"

"He was confident, brave, loyal — loyal to what he believed and to the people he loved. And he was strong, physically and willfully strong. He was a man who could do anything he put his mind to. Many men in Bree wanted to court your mother, you know. She had her choice of a few fine men, and she chose your father. He once said to my husband Mann, 'You'll see, within the year, I'm going to marry Lana ko Dir'."

"And he did? Within the year?"

"Yes," she laughed. "After that, Mann had a sense of awe about your father."

"And even back then father was rhyming."

"Yes, he had a gift for rhyme. He had an unusual brilliance. He was never a good reader, so he didn't do well in school. Instead, he put his attention into that which he was good at. He excelled at sports and was an exceptionally fast runner. In fact, after he graduated from Upper School, instead of becoming a fisherman with your grandfather, he worked as a runner for three years."

"Father was a runner?" I asked.

"You didn't know?"

"No." I imagined father running parcels from town to town. Had he ever run to Donnot?

"Then he took up fishing and that's when he first met your mother."

"Because her father fished."

"Yes."

"I was just thinking, Teacher Hana, how awful it was for father when he lost his leg. Not just the physical pain, but the pain of not being able to run anymore."

"Yes. His physical pain was excruciating for a while, but it eventually subsided. The loss of his strength as a man, though, that was so much more difficult for him, and I sense that he still struggles with it."

"I sense he does too," I said. "I know that's why his love and sweetness got buried. He was angry that it happened, and he's still not over it. And then losing mother.... It's so unfair," I said. "It's so completely unfair."

"It is, Lin, it is," she said. "I'm at a loss to understand why, but life is unfair to everyone."

"Everyone?"

"Everyone. Some more than others. But yes, everyone. Tell me, how is life at home these days?"

"With father and Aunt Tala?"

"Yes."

"Up and down. It's been better in some ways since Aunt Tala and I got back from the Embassy Island. She's ... we're getting along better."

"And your father?"

"Not so great lately. He hates hearing us talk about the Continentals and their technology. I think he's jealous."

"He may be. And how are the two of them getting along?"

"Like they always do. They argue. Not all the time, but at least once a week."

"I'm concerned for you, Lin."

"Me?"

"I worry about your home life."

"My family's gotten completely nutty."

"Yes," Teacher Hana said, "that's my concern. Completely nutty is not an ideal environment for a child to grow up in."

"She actually said 'completely nutty'?" Mira asked.

It was the first time she interrupted my Teacher Hana story with a comment. I realized in that moment what an excellent listener Mira was.

"Yes," I said, "she actually said it." I popped some wistberries in my mouth, which was dry from so much talking. "So," I said, "here's the answer to your question. The reason I'm having dinner at Teacher Hana's is that she's worried I'm missing out on good parenting. She wants me to be a part of a normal family."

"That's really kind of her," Mira said.

"Isn't it?"

"You'll be the envy of half the girls in Bree, you know."

"Why?"

"Don't you know that they're sweet on Bin?"

"Teacher Hana's son?"

Mira nodded.

"No, I didn't know at all. But don't tell them about our dinners," I said. "Don't tell anyone. You know how rumors go."

"I won't tell a soul."

"Can you believe my father was a runner?"

"I thought only Eglians were runners."

"Where'd you hear that?"

"It's been so long," Mira said, "I don't remember."

"Do you think my father would have run with Eglians?"

"No, I don't think they run together. I think they each have a route and they run it on their own."

"Maybe I'll ask him." I imagined asking my father about his days as a runner and quickly saw that it wouldn't go well. "Maybe I won't."

"Right," Mira said, "maybe you shouldn't. Speaking of runners, have you written to your friend Vola yet?"

"I did, I sent it yesterday. You'll never guess who mailed it for me."

"Jabe di Groot's great-grandfather," she said.

"How'd you know?"

"He's been sending the mail since forever."

"Want to hear what I wrote Vola?"

"Absolutely."

Dear Vola,

Your mother's package to my Aunt Tala arrived just one day after your letter did. It's amazing, isn't it, how much they have in common and how much you and I do? Except for my best friend Mira and our Elder's wife and my Nature School teacher, there isn't anyone in Bree who loves progress, goodness, and technology as much as you and me.

Tell your mother that I appreciate all the materials she sent about the International Schools. Aunt Tala has been reading about the application requirements, and I've been reading about everything else. Except I have to say, at first I only looked at the pictures. I've never seen such supremely beautiful beaches, especially compared to Bree Beach. I like the violet sands of the islands of Vona and Lida the best.

How do you think your interviews went? And when will you hear from the Application Committee? I'm rooting for you that they say yes, and as nice as your parents are and as intelligent and progress-minded as you are, I feel very confident you'll be accepted.

To answer your question, 4,500 people live in

Bree. That makes Donnot the size of three Brees!
No wonder you have more holophones than we do.
My father is a fisherman and someday I'll tell you
about my mother, who taught Lower School and
who is very loved by everyone.

Next week I'm competing in a school competition.
We have about eight of them a year. This one is the
Best Two-Minute Tail-Painted Sandpainting. Does
your school have competitions?

I hope to hear from you soon. If you'd like, I'll
write every week. It's only three pargens to send a
letter and I rather like the mail clerk, even though
he's a toothless old man.

To progress and goodness!

Your friend,

Lin

THE THROW-AWAY DAY

"Gonna need your raincape today!" Mira hollered when she appeared at our doorstep in the early morning. "It's raining buckets!"

"Rained all night," I heard Aunt Tala say.

"Oh, hi, Aunt Tala."

"Hello, Mira. Right on time, as always."

"I try to be."

"It's a very good quality," Aunt Tala said, "especially for keeping appointments."

"How's your bookkeeping work?"

"Better than it's ever been, I'm happy to say. Lin's running a little late this morning. All that rain and thunder last night, she didn't sleep very well."

"I don't mind waiting," Mira said.

I munched the last of my turo egg sandwich, threw my flasan raincape over my shoulders, and joined them in the portal.

"All right, you two, I'm off," Aunt Tala said with a bright smile and a straightening of her raincape, the pretty red one she wore for special occasions.

"Good luck," I told her. Then I turned to Mira. "She has an interview with Merchant Kam. He's looking for a new bookkeeper."

"Then good luck," said Mira.

"Thank you, girls. Keep dry today and watch for mudslides!"

Mira and I stood inside the front door and watched the rain pour from a thick blanket of low-hanging clouds. After carefully covering her ears with the hood of her raincape, Aunt Tala walked down the wet, wooden steps with uncharacteristic poise, then turned right toward the Upper Path. I said a simple prayer for the very best outcome, and a tiny tear of love fell from my eye.

"She's in good spirits today," Mira said.

"She is," I agreed, nodding my happiness for her. "If you're going to an interview, the best thing is to be in a good mood."

"Bet we're meeting today in the lightning shelter."

"Bet you're right," I said. "We'll know soon enough." We looked at each other and grinned. "Ready?"

"Ready."

We stepped out into the rain and hopped down the eight wooden steps to the Upper Path. Before I turned left, I stopped and looked to the right for Aunt Tala, but didn't see her. She'd already disappeared in a maze of dwellings and bushes, on the other side of which was the marketplace and the office of Merchant Kam.

"It feels like a krillion baby fitchi birds are dropping from the sky!" Mira cried as we bounded down the path.

"A krillion krillion!" I yelled.

"At least there's no sky-to-ground lightning! It's all in the clouds today!"

"That's joy to my ears," I hollered, which was no exaggeration. I had a larger than normal fear of sky-to-ground lightning ever since an old fisherman friend of father's was struck by lightning while out on his boat. It knocked him overboard, and he was never seen again. We all went to the funeral. Even though it happened six years ago, the memory was fresh in my mind, especially that part of the funeral when all the flowers were laid on his burial cloth. If father had known that mother, too, would die in the sea, he wouldn't have let her step one foot on a boat ever again.

"Hey, take a look," Mira said.

She was ten paces ahead of me, looking down at that spot on the beach where Nature School met every morning except on days of inclement weather. No one was there except for a few schoolmates who were slowly making their way to the lightning shelter.

"Why do I have the feeling it's going to be a throw-away day?" Mira said.

"A throw-away day?"

"You know, a day when we don't learn much and everyone's misbehaving and Teacher Hana can do little more than keep everyone in line."

"Oh," I said, "a throw-away day."

Mira was right, our schoolmates were restless. Teacher Hana was attending to an injured foot. A few boys were circled around her, gawking at the blood. Everyone else was strewn about the one-room, rock and mortar lightning shelter, indulging in their usual antics — pulling legs and wings off dead sea critters, doing tail tricks, throwing pebbles on the beach from the beach-view window, playing the game knock-me-over — which isn't easy to do when the tail is strategically used.

"Hey girls," said someone behind Mira and me. It was Bissa, who wiggled her way in between.

"Hey Bissa," we said.

Bissa laughed. "I rather like these days of mayhem."

"Mira's calling it a throw-away day."

"That'd be good," Bissa said. "I'm in no mood for learning."

"That'll get you far—"

Mira was cut off by three loud handclaps and the sound of Teacher Hana's voice.

"Let's circle, everyone!" she hollered above the noise. "Circle! Circle! Circle!" she clapped.

"Why don't we make it a play day since we can't be outside?" someone asked.

"I have a better idea," Teacher Hana said.

"What could be better than play?"

"How about a voyage to space?"

"Ooooo," some cooed.

"Lin's going to share with us her experiences at the Continental Embassy Island and the World Library," Teacher Hana announced.

Shouts and squeals bounced off the brick walls as I walked to the front of the lightning shelter and wondered what to say. I had a bit of a problem. It wasn't a problem of not knowing what to say; it was a problem of not knowing what to leave out. I had more stories than a school day could hold.

Teacher Hana helped me up on a flatrock on the north end of the lightning shelter. I steadied my footing and looked down at the sea of faces staring up at me.

"So this is what it's like to be a teacher," I said.

Everyone laughed, even Teacher Hana. My presentation was off to a good start.

***

"You warmed up the audience before casting your first net," father told me that night at dinner. He had never been so proud of me. "Got them good and warm. And you did it in the best way, with humor. If you get them laughing, you'll win their affection and even their loyalty."

Aunt Tala rolled her eyes.

"Tell me how they liked your talk," father asked.

"Well," I said, "they were pretty well behaved, especially for it being a throw-away day. That's a day where not much teaching or learning's going on. And most lightning shelter days are throw-away days. There were a couple of times when someone tried to poke fun, but Jabe di Groot shut them up. And that's kind of amazing since he's known as the meanest boy in school. But he's been getting nicer because he likes Teacher Hana and she's been a good influence on him. And he and I sort of became friends a while back. Now I think we're officially friends. We'll see. Time will tell."

"I would keep that friendship strong," father said. "You want to be on the good side of the mean boys." He nodded to seal the advice. "And when you finished, did they clap?"

"Father wanted to hear it all," I told Mira as we walked to school the next day. "I talked for two hours, and he listened the whole time. I've never felt more loved by him than last night."

"It's how it should be," Mira said. "He cared about what you had to say."

"And he wasn't shy about showing it. That was the best part. He kept saying, 'and what happened next?'"

"And do you think he got the full impression of what a great talk it was?"

"I think so," I said. "But you know what? That doesn't matter as much as how good it felt to have his attention and curiosity."

"Your father doesn't strike me as particularly curious."

"Curious? No. And you can believe me, Mira, I speak from experience."

Mira and I laughed. The rain had stopped early in the morning, so it would be a normal school day that day. When we arrived on the beach, we saw Teacher Hana standing at the Teaching Rock and a scattering of our schoolmates drawing pictures in the wet sand with the tips of their tails.

"They're practicing for the Two Minute Tail-Painted Sandpainting Competition," Mira said.

"Let's do too," I said, "after school today."

"Sounds good."

But that never happened, due to a surprising welcome. As Mira and I approached the Teaching Rock, we were spotted, and one by one, my classmates abandoned their sandpaintings and clapped for me.

"They supremely loved your talk," Mira said, "just like I said."

Class that day was another throw-away day, a day when we didn't learn much from Teacher Hana, when everyone was so distracted it required exhaustive effort for her to keep them in line. But being the excellent teacher she was, she decided to ditch her planned lesson and give my schoolmates the education they really deserved. They wanted to hear more about the Holographic Library. She devoted the school day to questions and answers. I sat on the Teaching Rock and answered questions. It was one of the most fun classes we ever had, even me who had to do all the work.

But it wasn't work, answering all the questions about the Embassy Island, the Continental people, clarkon, and outer space. It was pure joy. The purest joy I had ever known.

DESTINED

Mira and I sat on the edge of the pier, our feet dangling in the warm Strellin Sea, which was eerily calm.

"So, Lin," Mira said, holding her gaze on the far horizon, "I've been thinking — if you wanted to, you could be destined for greatness."

Lightning erupted, fierce but silent, and churning billows of purple-pink clouds were lit bright white from the inside out.

"Oooooo," cooed Mira and I and the others who had gathered on the beach and piers to watch one of the best lightning shows we'd seen in years. It was the best kind of storm — far enough not to bother us, but close enough to see.

"Destined for greatness?" I asked, touched by the thought of it. "What makes you say that?"

"Well," Mira said, "first you were famous after your mother won the Most Gently Effective Disciplinarian Competition. Then you were more famous after she died. Now you're even more famous because you're the first girl in Bree who's been to the Embassy Island."

"I guess you're right, Mira. Who would've thought?"

A thousand tendrils of white light spun out of a single, brilliant full-sky flash. It was so beautiful, my hair stood on end.

"So now that you're a celebrity," Mira said, "what are you going to do about it?"

"Celebrity," I laughed. "Isn't that a little exagerrated?"

"Not really. Everyone knows you now, everywhere you go. Not

just schoolmates, but adults. It's true," she says when I shake my head. "You're just being modest about your fame."

"I'd rather be modest than think I'm great because all the kids know me."

"I didn't say great, I said famous. You're too young to be great. I said you're *destined* to become great."

Three flashes filled the sky with a white so white I had to close my eyes.

"Ooooo!" the people cried.

"So," Mira said, "what are you going to do about it?"

"What's there to do?"

"Use your clout," she said.

"Clout?"

"Clout. Power. Influence. You're an influential person now. You have power over people."

"I don't want power over anyone."

"No, not like the way your father has power over you, that's not what I'm talking about. It's a bigger kind of power. You have the power to do something good for Bree. You can actually help change things. Father said the other night that men with good reputations can get things done. A lot of people know you and like you and trust you. You have a good reputation."

"Oh," I said, "I like that."

A brilliant golden light exploded inside the storm clouds.

"Mira! Did you see the golden light?"

"I did," she said.

"I love yellow-orange. It's such an uplifting color, don't you think?"

"It's pretty uplifting as far as colors go."

"Did I ever tell you I asked father for my seventh birthday to paint my sleepingroom yellow-orange?"

"No," she nodded.

"All the walls and the ceiling. He said, 'Why the color of bird poo?' I told him, 'I don't think of it as poo, I think of it as a golden sun.' And he said, 'Then why not paint a golden sun? It'll take a lot less paint.' And I said, 'If you just paint a big circle of gold on the wall, then it *will* look like bird poo.'"

Mira laughed, "A really big bird."

"A massive bird."

"A malmagni," she said, "they're big."

"I still want yellow-orange walls," I said. "Now more than ever. It'd cheer me up. Maybe I should ask father again."

"I'd be careful if I were you."

"You're right. He'd just say no. That's his favorite word with me."

"Hey, I just thought of an example," Mira said.

"Example of what?"

"How you could use your clout."

"My clout, right. What?"

"You could start a petition to re-elect new members of the Committee of Technology."

"Wouldn't that be great!"

"Wouldn't it?" Mira squeezed my arm. "So listen," she said, "this is how clout works. You have a petition to get something done, like to hold a new election for the Committee of Technology. To get signatures for your petition, you need to convince people that your issue is a worthy cause. You're the perfect person to do that. Everyone knows you're practically an expert on technology, so they'll think, 'Lin really knows what she's talking about when it comes to the Committee of Technology.' Everyone knows and likes you, so unless they're total haters of technology, they would definitely sign your petition."

"Mira, I think you're on to something."

She *was* on to something. As the days passed, I couldn't stop thinking about clout and petitions and doing something good for Bree. I loved Bree, as much as I hated its backwardness. And even though my visit to the Embassy Island made the backwardness more painful, I didn't dislike Bree the more for it. I felt sadness instead, a big sadness, which Teacher Hana told me was compassion.

One night when Aunt Tala and I were cooking and she was in a mood not to talk, I slipped into a daydream about the satellite broadcasts. I daydreamed that Bree had a satellite reception tower and everyone who wanted one had a holophone. If we had holophones and a satellite reception tower, we could see everything there was to see in the World Library. We could see lifelike moving pictures of the satellites and stars and planets and outer space and adibadis working in a garden and buku trees that glow in the dark. With satellite reception and holophones, we could visit places without ever leaving Bree: the moss deserts of Egli, the tall and jagged mountains that separated Northern and Southern Wershonia, the modern cities of the Continent, the geysers of Waturi, and every single island where a International School was located.

I dreamt this daydream whenever I was alone and at night before I fell asleep. I even nightdreamed it, more than once.

Lying in bed one night, when mother's presence was especially strong, I silently told her about it. A beautiful feeling filled my heart, a feeling of encouragement.

"Should I?" I asked mother.

"Yes," I felt from her. "Yes."

And that's when I decided to use this clout that Mira was so supremely confident I had. I was going to start a petition to get satellite broadcast reception in Bree so we could have holophones and learn about the world.

Two nights later was my Nadri night dinner with Teacher Hana's family. I thought it best to tell them about it first.

"Mr. ni Ru," I asked her husband, "what do you know about petitions?"

"Are you asking what they are or how they work?" he asked.

"I want to know how to make one."

"You want to make a petition?"

"I've been thinking about it."

"A petition for what?"

"A petition to get satellite broadcast reception in Bree."

"That's quite ambitious."

"But isn't that what petitions are for? If you want something to change, it doesn't just change on its own. You have to do something about it. What if I'm not the only one who wants Bree to get the satellite broadcasts? What if a lot of people want it? If we don't say anything or do anything about it, then the Committee of No Technology will get their way."

"The Committee of No Technology?" asked Mr. ni Ru. "Is that a joke?"

Dabi and Bin were giggling.

"Sort of," I said. "It's a joke with a meaning."

"It's very funny," he said.

"Then you agree with me," I told him. "Don't they seem to be against technology?"

"They're against rapid change."

"They must think any change is rapid change," I told him. "But that would make sense. They're all old."

"They are," said Bin, who had just turned 14. "I'd sign your petition."

"Me too," said his little sister Dabi.

"Well, I would sign your petition," said Mr. ni Ru, "and there are others I know who would enthusiastically do the same."

"Have you talked with anyone else about your idea?" Teacher Hana asked.

"No, not yet. I wanted to ask all of you first. I trust your knowledge and opinions."

"Do you feel strongly about this?" Mr. ni Ru asked. "Strongly enough to commit to the petition project and see it through?"

"I have supremely strong feelings about bringing the satellite broadcasts to Bree," I said. "And once I started the petition, my interest in it would only grow stronger, I'm sure of it."

"You'd be surprised how many people want satellite reception," Bin said. "But they don't think there's anything they can do about it."

"Yet signing a petition is something they *could* do," said Mr. ni Ru.

"You're doing all the work for them, Lin, by initiating the petition. All they have to do is sign their agreement."

"Initiating the petition," I said. "I like the sound of that. So how do I do it?"

"I'm not quite sure what the process is," he said, "but I could pay a visit to the Mayor's Office."

"You would?"

"Of course, I'd be glad to."

Less than two weeks later, I had good news for mother.

"It's really real, mother!" I silently told her as I curled up for sleep that night. "I'm holding it in my hands right now, the actual petition! It's the same kind of petition that grown-ups use to get things done. The Mayor's secretary was very nice to me. Mr. ni Ru took me there, and she was surprised that the petition was my doing, not his. She said to him, 'You must be very proud of your daughter', which made us laugh and laugh. I laugh a lot with the ni Ru's. They're the best family I know, loving and kind and generous and helpful. Maybe that's why they laugh so much. I'm learning what it is to have a brother and sister, and I like it, I love it. It's like I have two families, mother, two families! I missed you as much today as yesterday and last week, but I'm getting better at not feeling sad. Instead, I remember a happy memory of you, and if Mira's around, I tell her about it. She's always loved you. My dreams are getting better. Last night I dreamt that I took you to the Continental Embassy. We had the best time two people can have. I wonder what I'll dream about tonight. I hope it's good, and I hope you're with me. I love you, mother, with all my heart."

CULTI RUINS THE DAY

Dear Vola,

Our petition is going well, better than I hoped. In only six days we're almost halfway to our goal of 1,000 signatures. We collected 189 just today due to Elder Evig's announcement at the end of his Adri service. It's a good sign for Bree that our elder is a true evolutionary.

Speaking of evolutionaries, turns out Mira and I aren't the only ones in Bree who are progress-minded. We just started a club called the Evolutionaries and have 8 members. I'll tell you more about it next time I write.

When I told Mira that the people of Donnot already know Culti, she about fell off her flatrock. No one knows Culti here, and a lot of adults are really annoyed that they have to learn it.

I was annoyed at first, but now I'm totally in favor of learning Culti. The way I see it, it's for progress. Plus, when I travel to the modern cities of the North some day I want to talk to people in their own language. World travel is one of my favorite daydreams, though I'm so busy with the petition, I don't have as much time for daydreams as I used to.

Have a good week at school and write when you can.
Your friend and fellow evolutionary,
Lin

Father pounded his fist on the dinner table. "And what's wrong with Welbi? It's a *fine* language! There's nothing wrong with it, nothing at all!"

Father was so agitated, he was swallowing his fishcakes whole. I wanted to remind him that he needs to chew if he doesn't want a stomach ache later, but I feared he wouldn't appreciate my good intentions with the mood he was in. Mother could tell him such things no matter what his mood, and he always took it well. She used a certain kind of sweetness that made him melt a little and follow her advice and even be grateful for it. But I wasn't mother, so I kept quiet.

"It's not that Welbi's an inferior language," said Grandmother Min, "it's just spoken by fewer people. If you want a single Wershonian language, then it makes sense for it to be Culti."

"It's a lot of trouble for an entire country to learn a new language," father said.

Grandmother Min put more kriddle fishcakes on his plate. "Most of Strellin speaks Culti already," she told him.

"*Most* of Strellin?" father asked.

"Only Bree and a few nearby villages don't teach Culti."

"We're more backward than I thought," I mumbled.

"What did you say, dear?"

"Nothing."

"And who gets to decide that we need a single language?"

"It was decided by the Co-National Assembly," said Grandmother Min, "which has 12 representatives from Strellin."

"But none from Bree," father muttered.

"No one from Bree wanted the job," said Grandfather Daun.

This conversation was going nowhere. And after the great day it had been, our family dinner was a sore disappointment. It was Kodri night and Aunt Tala was at a special dance that the merchants put on every month. If I'd been old enough, Aunt Tala said she would have let me go with her. But as it was, I was stuck with father and my grandparents for the night. I wondered if this is what father's Nadri night dinners were like when I ate at Teacher Hana's. Bickering with his parents. What a sorry rut.

"Can't force a man to learn a new language," father said, "I don't care what their good reasons are. I see no need to learn Culti, and I'm not going to do it."

What happened to father? Only ten minutes ago he was laughing and happy. He'd been happy in the morning and all through the day. It was his happiest day since mother died. And it mostly had to do with me.

That morning, father came to Elder Evig's service. He went without coaxing or pleading. He went because he wanted to. He wanted to see what all the fuss was over my petition. And once he was there, he was glad he went. He liked seeing my popularity with everyone, he liked hearing Elder Evig take a minute before the last song to announce my petition, and he liked seeing the swarm of people who gathered at Bree Pavillion to sign my petition and ask me questions about the satellite broadcasts.

Father was proud of me that day, just like he was on that throw-away day when I stood up on a flatrock in the lightning shelter and taught my schoolmates about technology and the world. Father was a proud man, and when his wife or daughter made him proud, it was just as good as being proud of himself. Maybe in his mind there was no difference.

When I arrived home late that afternoon with the 189 signatures we collected that day, father wanted to see them all. He unclipped my stack of petition papers, spread them out on the dining table, and stood back to look at them in admiration.

"You did this!" he said. "All on your own!" He kissed me on the head. "Did you see the respect everyone had for you?"

"Yes," I said, "the adults take me a lot more seriously now."

"I'm very proud of you, Lin. I wish your mother could be here to see it."

"I'm glad *you're* here, father. And I'm glad you're proud of me." I wrapped my arms around his waist and laid my head on his belly, which wasn't rotund like some of the other fishermen. I squeezed him tight and luxuriated in the warmth I felt from him. His inner sanctum of sweetness had never shone so bright. "I love you, father," I said.

"I love you too, Lin. You're a good girl. And I'm very, very proud of you." He let me hug him for the longest time.

"You know, father," I finally said, "Aunt Tala's going to the Merchant's Dance tonight. We won't be eating dinner with her."

"Then we'll have dinner with your grandparents," he said.

"Do you think I should help Grandmother Min in the kitchen?"

"I think you should rest or read or play," father said. "Do something you enjoy. You've had a busy weekend, and you have school in the morning."

Positive pride sure had a good effect on father. I was surprised by his kindness and advice, but didn't let on about it. If I did, he might have snapped back to his old ways. So I acted normal instead, and that made it more fun — him acting normally and me acting normally, together. I hoped and believed it was the beginning of greater sweetness between us. Maybe all I had to do was make him proud of me.

When we sat down for dinner at Grandmother Min's softwood table, we were all in a good mood from the day, and father was especially talkative. He went on about my popularity and laughed and laughed as he retold Elder Evig's talk, which was more humorous than usual with his story about the two fishermen who were fishing in the dark, one with a net and one with a bucket and some faith.

"The one with the net was the smarter one," father said when he finished the story.

"Faith is good for a lot of things," I said, "but it won't make fish jump in a bucket."

Father laughed. "Fish jumping in a bucket, now that I'd like to see."

"Imagine, Jorn, if you had that command over fish," grinned Grandfather Daun.

"I'd be a rich man!" father declared. "And no worse for wear."

I wanted to talk more about faith, which Elder Evig said is the belief in goodness, but how could I steer the conversation from making fish jump in a bucket to believing in goodness? It seemed too far a leap. But that was all right, another idea came into my mind, and it was fairly evolutionary.

"Let's count how many people father saw today who he knows and likes," I said.

Father took to the idea, and it became an enjoyable game where father voted yay or nay on the names my grandparents and I called out. He offered a few of his own, and when the game was finished, I was cheered to find that father liked at least ten people in Bree. Grandmother Min brought me some paper so I could write the names down for a secret future purpose. Father could use a few good friends, and this list would be very valuable.

I'd never had such a good time with my father and grandparents as that night. It could have gone down in history as our finest and funnest, but that was forever ruined when Grandfather Daun, who's not the most skillful socializer, brought up the big announcement that Culti was now the official language of all of Wershonia and we would have to learn it. Father pounded his fist on the table, and that was that.

Impressioned

"Aunt Tala, you're all out of breath!"

She dropped a heavy slingbag to the floor and stared at me, head shaking with disappointment. What was I in trouble for now? I followed her into the kitchen, filling fast with dread.

"How about some tichi tea?" I asked.

"That'd be great, Lin."

While I made her tea, Aunt Tala paced the kitchen and told me the news.

"I was buying fish at the pier," she said, "and overheard some of the fishermen talking about your petition."

"My petition? Why?"

"They're against it."

"Maybe they've been talking to Califer Crigs," I said. "He's been saying I'm a bad influence. I saw him yesterday. He shook his crooked, scabbed-up finger in my face and scared me so bad I thought for sure I'd start having nightmares again."

Aunt Tala frowned at me. "Califer Crigs," she said. "You be careful there. Don't tangle with him. He hasn't been right since that mudslide killed his wife."

"I know. And sure he's going to be against my petition. He's just a crazy old coot who hates progress because he hates everything."

"Well," she shook her head, all grim and serious, "he's not the only one. There are others who aren't happy with what you're doing."

"How many do you think?"

"Your guess is as good as mine."

"Well, they don't have to sign the petition," I said. "They can have their opinion."

"That's fine and sporting of you Lin, but it's not that simple."

"Sure it is."

"No, it's not. There's more."

I gave Aunt Tala her tea, sat at the kitchen table, and listened.

"They weren't saying very nice things about *you*," she said.

"What kind of things?"

"That you're corrupting the youth of Bree and upsetting our way of life. Bringing Bree to ruin. Things like that."

Aunt Tala only stopped pacing to sip her tea. For once I was the calm one.

"You're right," I said, "that's pretty bad."

"It gets worse."

"Worse?"

"Your father was there," she said as a cold queasiness filled my belly. "At first he didn't say anything at all, like the coward that he is. But then someone insulted you and got twisted in a fit. He shouted at them never to talk bad about you like that."

"He did?" I couldn't help but smile, and the cold queasy turned warm.

"He did, I saw all of it."

"But he didn't see you."

"No," she said.

"What happened then?"

"Some of them started taunting your father, accusing him of being too lenient and aiding and abetting your seditious behavior."

"Seditious?"

"Traitorous. They think your petitions are akin to treason. They said your father's a traitor to Bree and the whole family should be put on trial and jailed."

"Jailed?"

"Don't worry, Lin. That will never happen. Everything they're saying is nonsense. I didn't want to tell you these things, but you're going to hear them eventually, and you need to be prepared."

"They're going to poison father's thinking with all that talk, Aunt Tala. This is terrible! Supremely, ultimately terrible! What are we going to do?"

"As for them, nothing. For your father, you need to be on your best behavior. Be more helpful and kind, but not too much. When his feelings are hurt, he can get in a nasty mood."

"I guess I shouldn't talk about how many signatures we got today."

"Don't say anything about your petition or holophones or the Continent or any of that."

"Right. Just be nice and sweet. I can do that. By the way, 57."

"What?"

"We got 57 signatures today."

"I'm happy for you, Lin. Now is there anything else you need to say to get it out of your head so you don't blurt it out at dinner and cause a scene?"

I thought about it, and I did. "We're official," I told her. "Our new club. The Evolutionaries. We had our first meeting yesterday after school. We decided we would meet every Kodri after school. Even though that's a time for getting signatures at the Teaching Rock, it's the least busy day because of the new shipments that come to market. Anyone can come to a meeting, but to be a member—"

"All right, that's good, Lin. You can tell me the rest later. Just don't talk about your club anywhere in father's presence for a while."

"How long do you think?"

"It all depends on him."

"Don't deprive him of his kono root. It will only make things worse. Promise, Aunt Tala?"

"Promise," she said half-heartedly.

"You have to say it like you mean it, or I won't believe you."

"I promise, Lin. I promise I won't deprive your father of kono. Is that good enough?"

"That was good."

"All right," she said, "let's put the shopping away and start dinner. I bought some stufferfish."

"That'll make father happy. Bissa gave me a bunch of wistberries. I could make another wistberry pie. He loved it, remember?"

"All right, good. You're in charge of that."

Despite the dire circumstances, Aunt Tala was in a mood to talk as we cooked. She had good news.

"Good news and bad news in one day," I said. "Why does it have to happen that way?"

"You'll see, Lin, as you grow up, that it's all a big mix. Sometimes your day is good, sometimes it's bad, but usually it has a measure of both. It's random."

"Oh. So I'm ready to hear your good news."

"I saw Merchant Kam today. He wants to hire me to be his full-time bookkeeper."

"You got the job!" I was happy for her, but I exaggerated my joy to help put her in a better mood. As Elder Evig often said at Adri service, "Love and joy are infectious."

As I'd hoped, my exaggerations were helping. She laughed with me and let out a squeal. It was a terrible squeal — and made me wonder if that's why adults never squealed, they just didn't know how to anymore — but at least she tried. She was in the spirit of celebration, and that was all that mattered.

"What's all this loud commotion going on?!" It was father. "No thumping, Lin. How many times do I have to tell you?"

In one small moment, our joyful celebration deflated like a dying pufferfish. Father was in a rotten mood, just as Aunt Tala predicted.

I had promised to be supremely nice, so I said the first nice thing I could think of. "We're making stufferfish and wistberry pie for dinner. Do you want to rest with some kono root until it's ready?"

He looked at me long and hard with steady, squinty eyes and no smile, no words, no kindness. I'd have given all the money I had to know what he was thinking. Did he hate me for causing his friends to taunt him? Did he hate them for saying such mean things about me? Was he wishing I had drowned and not mother?

"Yes, Jorn," Aunt Tala said, "how about a rest before dinner?"

"How about you two telling me what's going on?"

"What do you mean, 'what's going on?'"

"Don't play games with me, Tala. You're hiding something. I can smell it. Just tell me what's going on."

"Aunt Tala got some good news today," I said.

"Good news?" father asked. "What kind of good news?"

"Merchant Kam has offered me the job."

Father's eyes turned bright. "That *is* good news, Tala. Congratulations. What'd you tell him?"

"That I would give him my answer tomorrow."

"Tomorrow!" he said. "Are you a fool? What if there's no job tomorrow?"

"He assured me there would be," Aunt Tala said.

"So why not just say yes to him now?"

"Because it's a full-time position with great responsibility. I can't keep my current clients if I work for him. I need to make arrangements."

"Does he know that?"

"Yes," she said, "and he said he appreciates my respect for my clients, my integrity, and my whole manner of handling it."

"Are you right about that?"

"Yes, Jorn, I am."

"Well, then," he said, "congratulations."

"Thank you."

Father looked at me again. The same look with the same stone eyes that were impossible to read. *I'm cooked,* I thought.

"I'll have some kono, Tala, and I'll have a rest."

"Go on, then," she said, "I'll bring it to you."

Father turned and limped to his sleepingroom.

Never had I thought a daydream-nightmare was possible, but if you put silence and fear together in the head, it can happen. Aunt Tala and I finished making dinner in total silence for obvious reasons, and in the empty quiet, my imagination tormented me with scenes of father's outrage. He yelled at me, "You're forbidden from writing Vola, from ever petitioning for anything ever again, and from all club activities! Forever!" He disowned me with cruel words, "You're a freak of nature and no child of mine!" And worst of all, he tore up my petition in a krillion pieces.

***

"It was the worst night of my life," I told Mira and Bissa the next morning before school. "I really didn't think I'd survive it. It's one thing for father to be angry and yell because I'm misbehaving or his leg hurts, but this is a whole new kind of angry. His friends think I'm a corrupter and a menace and who knows how long they'll keep giving him grief about it. I fear for my future."

"Tell us what happened at dinner," Bissa said.

"Nothing," I said. "That's the problem. He wouldn't look at me or talk to me. I wanted to be nice, but I was too afraid to say anything to him. So I mostly said nothing. Aunt Tala was nice and tried to make cheery chit chat, but that didn't help. He said he wasn't in the mood to talk. After dinner, he went straight to his sleepingroom."

"Did you see him this morning?" Mira asked.

"No, he was up early."

"What are you going to do?"

"I'm going to keep asking my voice of reason what love would do."

Mira nodded. "That sounds good."

"Does that work?" Bissa asked. "Do you ever get an answer?"

"I think sometimes I do, with easy stuff. But with the hard things, like father, I never know."

"I don't envy you, Lin," Mira told me.

"Me neither," said Bissa. "What an awful father."

"He's not awful," I said, "he's broken. He's lost without mother."

"You lost her too and you're not angry and mean," Bissa said.

"Sure, but I'm not maimed from an unfair act of nature."

"Good point."

Mira took my hand and squeezed some love into it. "You'll get through this, Lin. We're here to help."

"Right," Bissa said, "and we wish you luck." She squeezed my other hand, tighter than she should have. Didn't she know love can't pass through a tight squeeze?

"I'll be all right," I said. "The real luck I need — the luck we need — is getting signatures. That's what I care about most. What's our total count now, Mira?"

She looked in her kipper-paper notebook. "Six hundred and forty-two."

"More than 350 to go," I said, empty of optimism. "Our numbers aren't as high this week as they should be."

"Be patient," said Mira. "We will get our thousand signatures, we just don't know how long it'll take."

It seemed a sign of good luck when Aunt Tala told me two days later that Merchant Kam wanted to sign our petition.

"He has a holophone," she said, "and he wants to—"

"Merchant Kam has a holophone?"

"Yes. And he—"

"A holophone?"

"Yes, Lin. Will you let me finish my sentence before your father gets home?"

It was impossible to let her finish. This news was monumental. "I didn't know that anyone in Bree owned a holophone," I told her. "What else don't I know about? And why didn't you ever mention it?"

"You never asked."

"Yes, but you knew—"

"Do you want him to sign your petition or not?"

"Yes, yes! Of course I do!"

"Then be silent and let me speak."

I put a towel in my mouth and started whipping the turo eggs.

"Merchant Kam can't use his holophone here for obvious reasons," she said, "so he's extremely pleased about your petition. He wants to sign it, and he wants to meet you. I'm going to his office tomorrow. He said to bring you along with your petition." She paused a long time, but I remained quiet. "Problem is, it's during school hours. We'll have to get special permission from Teacher Hana to excuse you from class." She paused again. "All right, Lin, you can speak now."

I unstuffed my mouth and faked being so out of breath I had to gasp for air. Aunt Tala threw a sprinkling of asi flour at me, which landed on my ears and face.

"Now I know what you'll look like in 80 years," she laughed. "You're going to be a darling old woman when your hair turns."

I dipped my hand in the asi flour and sprinkled more on the other side of my face. "There, now I'm completely old! Older than Grandmother Min!"

Aunt Tala's laughter trailed off and her natural seriousness returned. "All right," she said, "hand me that salt."

"I can't believe Merchant Kam has a holophone," I said. "What a mystery man. Why does he have a holophone if he lives in Bree?"

"He travels up North and uses it there."

"I can't wait to meet him," I said. "I have so many questions."

"Easy on the questions, Lin. He's a busy man. Let him ask the questions, all right?"

"You know he's the most rumored-about person in all of Bree."

"Lin, I'm not joking about this. Don't assault him with questions or too much talking."

"All right."

"Say it like you understand it and mean it. Do you realize how important it is to me that this meeting go well with him? If you mess it up, I'll never...."

"You'll never what?"

She thought before answering. "I'll never have that kind of opportunity again."

From the tone of her voice, I sensed she meant, "I'll never forgive you", and I was glad she didn't say it. I was proud of her for hesitating and saying a better thing, even if it wasn't true. More and more, her inner sanctum of sweetness was influencing her behavior, and it was making her a better person.

Wanting to be a better person myself, I thought it best to tell her that I understood the importance of her meeting with Merchant Kam and that I not ruin it.

Aunt Tala smiled and love-tugged my ear. "Thank you, Lin. To tell you the truth, I'm a bit nervous, and your being there will be a comfort to me." "I hope I'm a comfort, and I hope—"

We both heard it, the sound of father's footsteps on the path outside the open window. His limp gave a signature sound that would forever prevent him from sneaking up on anyone or showing up to a place unrecognized. He turned from the path onto the stair steps that lead to our front door. Aunt Tala and I were seized with panic.

"Father!"

"Your face!"

Aunt Tala wiped my face furiously with a dry diningcloth. Flour flew in my eyes and ears and it tickled. I tried hard not to laugh and snorted instead, which made me laugh anyway. The front door opened and closed. Aunt Tala checked my face and rubbed a spot she missed. As father's footsteps approached the kitchen, Aunt Tala and I took to our cooking, pretending to be normal, as if nothing unusual had happened — no talk of Merchant Kam and holophones, no flour in my face, no hysterical laughter, nothing but cooking.

When we sat down to dinner, Aunt Tala and I had little to say. We were both thinking about Merchant Kam and our meeting with him the next morning. Aunt Tala had given father a double dose of kono root when he got home, and he too was quiet, happily so.

And the three of us had dinner in silence, each happy for our own reason.

THE SPECIAL SIGNATURE

I slipped out early, quietly out the back door while everyone was singing.

Mira saw me and winked knowingly. "I'll see you there," she mouthed with more embellishment than the moment required. She was out of her mind happy. I was too, mostly. Mother was on my mind, she was all that was missing from this nearly perfect day. She and father.

Bree Pavillion was massive when empty. I laid down on a flatrock table, closed my eyes, and roamed my heart for mother's presence, which was strong and quick to rise. Practice had made finding her more easy.

"I wish you could be here," I said to her silently. "I think this is going to be a very important day."

In the distance, the back door of the Assembly Hall flew open. Shouts erupted, happy ones. And then I heard them, my fellow Evolutionaries, leaping through the door like a pack of caged loupits. They ran across the mossy field that stretched between the Assembly Hall and Bree Pavillion.

Dabi, the fastest, was first to arrive. "They clapped!" she shouted. "Lin, they clapped for our petition!"

I said goodbye to mother and opened my tear-bleary eyes.

"They clapped," I said, less happy than I should have been.

My eyes focused on the dingy brown flasan tent-top, so thick and opaque it completely blocked the view of the sky. I imagined a clarkon canopy there in its place, so completely invisible you'd see the entire sky and every shape and color and movement of the clouds. You could watch lightning right above you in total safety. I smiled and wondered how much a clarkon canopy for Bree Pavillion would cost.

Mira and Hali bounded breathlessly in, carrying slingbags of petitions, writingboards, kipper-ink pens, and wistberries.

Bissa took charge of the organization of our materials and neatly arranged the petitions and pens on the flatrock table where the signers would sign. Mira sat on one of the tables and wrote notes in her kipper-paper notebook. She was planning to write a long news article about our petition drive. "Maybe the Strellin newspaper will print it," she told me not long ago. One month later, they did.

"Here they come!" Dabi hollered.

I drew a big breath. "Ready everyone?"

"Ready!"

Our tails thumped as we waited, our little club of Evolutionaries. I felt proud and hopeful.

The crowd around us grew quickly thick. Many in the crowd had already signed, but came to show their support and to see how we were doing that day. I realized we should keep a running count so we would know exactly when we got the one-thousandth signature.

I whistled like some of the old fishermen do and shouted, "Hali!" He stood up on a table and saw me. I motioned him over.

"Hali," I said, "will you keep a tally of all the signatures we get today? We need 39 to reach our goal. I want to know when we have 30. Will you do that for me?"

"Sure, Lin."

"Lin!" I heard behind me. I spun around and saw Aunt Tala, Grandmother Min, and Grandfather Daun.

"Did you hear?" I said. "Only 39!"

"We're so proud, Lin," Aunt Tala said.

"Very proud," agreed Grandmother Min.

"If I could sign twice," said Grandfather Daun. "I would."

"I'd let you be the thousandth," I told him. "That will be a special signature today."

"Wish he could sign for your father," Aunt Tala said.

"Where is father?" I asked. "Did he come today?"

Aunt Tala shook her head. "No, Lin. I'm sorry. He's in a mood."

I smiled to hide my sadness.

"Don't be hurt," said Grandmother Min. "It's his fear and pride."

My sadness over father's no-show was small compared to the love I felt from Aunt Tala and my grandparents and everyone else who spoke to me that day of their gratitude for what we were doing. Despite the attempts of the naysayers to turn people against the petition through fear-mongering and false opinionating, more people wanted satellite broadcast reception than didn't.

I went looking for Hali, who stood behind the line of rapid signature gathering.

"Hali," I asked, "where are we?"

"We've got 29 signatures," he grinned, "probably a couple more than that by now."

"All right," I said, "At 38 signatures, tell the girls to stop. We'll be just one signature away from our goal. It'll be a special moment, and I want to make an announcement. And I want the thousandth signature to be a special person. I don't know who, we'll just see who's around who hasn't signed yet."

"I'll tell them," Hali said before he turned and skipped away.

As I waited for the 38th signature to be signed, I saw Jabe di Groot. I smiled and waved and he smiled back, a friendly smile. Next to Jabe stood his great-grandfather, that sweet old man who mailed my letters to Vola every week. I made my way toward them through the crowd. I wanted to say a quick hello before it was time to make my announcement.

"Hey, Lin," said Jabe. He held out his arm for an elbow bump.

"Hey, Jabe," I said. We bumped elbows. Great-grandfather di Groot toothlessly chuckled.

"Hi, Mr. di Groot," I said.

"Hello, Lin. You got a pretty good turnout today."

"All the Adri's have been good," I said, "thanks to Elder Evig. He's been mentioning the petition at the end of every assembly."

"Sends them all straight to you," he said.

"Yes," I said, "I suppose he does."

Great-grandfather di Groot coughed his cough and said, "I came today myself to sign your petition."

"You haven't signed yet?"

"No. Not that I didn't want to. Just don't make it out this side of town too much."

"Would you like the honor of being the thousandth signature?" I asked him. Jabe smiled at the idea.

"Is that the winning signature?" Great-grandfather di Groot asked.

"It is! The winning signature. It would mean a lot to me if it was you."

"Well," he said, "what a great privilege. An honor it would be. You just tell me when I should take my turn."

"Any time now," I said. "Here, follow me."

Great-grandfather di Groot followed me through the crowd to the front of the four signature-signing lines. I noticed, for the first time that day, how festive the mood was. The folks in line didn't look at all impatient. They and the onlookers were chatting and laughing as if at the annual Bree Beach Party. *This is the day Bree changes forever*, I thought. My heart beat so fast, I thought it might burst. More than once I felt that it had, with streams of golden-yellow love that exploded outward in every direction, touching every single person in the world. Even the naysayers.

We reached the front of the signing lines.

"Wait right here," I said to Great-grandfather di Groot.

I looked for Hali to see how were doing, but I didn't need to ask.

"We got it, Lin!" Mira shouted. We had our 999 signatures.

"Hali, help me up on the table."

I put my hand on Hali's shoulder and hopped up on the table that had been our central petition-collecting location for the last three

Adri's. I whistled a few times, as loud as I could. Everything moved in super slow-motion, which I was happy for since it was one of the most monumentally important moments of my life.

"I have an announcement to make!" I shouted to the crowd, which had not grown smaller with the collecting of signatures like all the other Adri's. Today, people signed and stayed. "We're just one signature away from satellite broadcast reception!"

The crowd cheered and clapped and hollered.

I looked down at Great-grandfather di Groot. "Are you ready?"

"I'm ready," he said.

I trembled as I watched Great-grandfather di Groot sign the petition on Mira's clipboard. How fitting it was that Bree was modernized and forever changed by the shaky scribble of this simple, old man who sent my letters of hope and progress to Vola and who connected Bree to the rest of the world with carrier birds and runners.

We would now be connected to the world holographically, in pictures and moving images, using a technology that no one in Bree could begin to understand.

Even though I was heartbroken that mother and father weren't there, it was still the greatest and happiest day of my life. Just as Aunt Tala said, the awful and the wonderful almost always go together. But the wonderful, I believed, was always the bigger cut of the fish.

SHINY SILVER PAPER

Two months passed, and as life so inconveniently does, the good and the bad sloppily mixed together in the unfolding story of my life, which could not be called supremely great nor hopelessly dreadful. It was always some of both.

Hopelessly dreadfully speaking, father was still hardly talking to me. When he did, he'd tell me that I was making his life miserable or that I was an embarrassment to our family or that I was going too far and needed some reigning in. I would tell him how much he was hurting me with his words and that I was already hurting bad enough from missing mother and that I knew he was hurting too, and since we were both hurting, shouldn't we have compassion for each other?

At times I felt him soften. But my pleas of love weren't enough to undo the insults and taunting he got all day from his fishermen friends at the pier who had been against my petition and now were against the Evolutionaries, my club of goodness. These anti-evolutionaries were small in number, and the way I saw it, father was listening too much to them and if his life was miserable, it was as much the fault of his narrow-mindedness than anything I was doing.

Bree had become divided, father said. But was that really true? Most people didn't think there was any divide at all, just a small band of naysayers who loudly opinionated any chance they saw fit. I agreed with father that there *was* a divide, but it wasn't between these people of Bree and those people of Bree. The divide, as I saw it, was between father and me. A wall stood between us, a wall of silence. It hurt, and I hated it. I wondered if father hated it too.

On the supremely great side of life, Aunt Tala was thriving in her new job with Merchant Kam, Vola got word that she was accepted to the International Schools, the Evolutionaries had three service projects underway, and Mira's story about our petition drive for satellite broadcast reception was published in *The Strellin National Recorder*, the biggest newspaper in our country, not a single copy of which had ever been delivered to Bree.

Teacher Tril's husband bought three copies of the paper on his next business trip to Tobbs. For weeks and weeks, these three copies were passed all around Bree. Everyone knew Mira now, making her famous like me and loved by everyone who felt proud that Bree was now known by all of Strellin.

Some say success and fame change people, and not always for the best. But Mira was changed, and it *was* for the best. I knew it the day she told me, "I have a bent ear, so what? I can write! I'm intelligent! I have a massive imagination and a gift for story writing. If a bent ear is the price I pay for my talent, then so be it." I was glad for Mira, but I didn't agree with her reasoning. I believed that talent was free and physical defects just plain bad luck.

On top of all the goodness going on, Bree would soon be outfitted with satellite broadcast reception! Two weeks after my petition was presented to the Mayor's Office for his seal of approval, Teacher Tril and her husband traveled to the Embassy Island to make arrangements for the installation of the receiving tower. I sorely wanted to go with them, and they asked me if I would, but I knew better not to ask father.

Teacher Tril and her husband returned with entertaining stories and a piece of silver shiny paper that just about everyone — even some of the naysayers — wanted to see and touch.

"It's just paper," I told Mira. "Wait 'til Bree gets some clarkon. That'll be something to thump your tail about."

"But it's silver and shiny," she said, "not at all like kipper-paper."

Rumors soon spread that the shiny silver paper had extraordinary, super-physical powers.

The paper was kept just outside the Mayor's Office, pinned to the wall of announcements at the entrance of Bree's biggest building, made centuries ago of orange stone. Due to its size and color, everyone called this building the Big Orange. It was a place few people went unless they needed a permit for a new boat or wanted to hear the Village Council debate laws or had a flooding problem to report to the Water Works Department. It was where the Committee of No Technology met once a month to deprive Bree of technological progress, and it was where lawyers took troublemakers to present their case to the Court of the Wronged and the Accused.

No one otherwise took interest in the Big Orange until the shiny silver paper appeared there one Bisri morning. After that, people lined up to see and touch the paper for themselves. Some believed the rumor that touching it would heal illness, and before long, the paper had been touched so much it was turning torn and ragged. Some thoughtless people would tear off a corner to take home. The Mayor soon put a stop to all of that. He appointed a rotation of security guards to stand next to the paper and keep everyone from touching it. "You can look only, nothing more," they were instructed to say. Even though they couldn't touch the shiny silver paper, people still came to look at it.

I wasn't interested in the paper's shininess or silveryness or the powers I knew it didn't have. I was interested in what was printed on it. The words were written in Welbi, in dark blue letters:

SATELLITE RECEIVING TOWER
INSTALLATION PROCEDURE

Town of Bree in Strellin of Wershonia

Installation will commence on
Bisri 13 Taso 2294 at the 7th Hour

The 13th of Bisri in the cool month of Taso. That was the day the Continentals would arrive and forever modernize Bree, a day that would go down in history. And when everyone finally tired of talking about the shiny silver paper, they started talking about the 13th of Bisri, naysayers included. They took to meeting in secret to discuss "what to do about the tower problem," as Hali had overheard. We all knew the naysayers were up to no good, but what kind of no good remained a top-secret mystery.

As for father, it turns out that even if you're against something and refuse to talk about it, that doesn't mean you're not curious. And on the 13th of Bisri, father left his fishing and stood on Bree Beach with his naysayer friends to see for himself this supremely epic history-making event.

THE DAY THEY CAME

Bree Beach was filling fast with onlookers.

My schoolmates, most of us, arrived early at the Teaching Rock. No adults were near, which contributed to the annoying incidents of pranks, bickering, and stupid conversations that all threatened to trivialize this monumental day.

"Did I miss anything?" Taun asked when he showed up.

"No," Mira said, "nothing's happened yet."

"When *will* something happen?" moaned a boy behind us.

"At the 7th Hour," I turned and said. "Didn't you read the announcement?"

"Saw it but didn't read it," he replied.

"How will we know when it's the 7th Hour?" asked the boy's cousin.

"When they show up," Bissa said.

"I hope they're not late," whined Jini Mae. "It's cold out here."

"You call this cold?"

"My ears are sensitive."

"Then put a raincape on your head."

"How can your minds be filled with such petty drivel?" I said. "They'll start when they start, and you'll know when that is, believe me, you'll know."

"Don't need to get all snippy, Lin," sneered Kon, once the second meanest boy in school and now the most mean.

Jabe di Groot, who was hardly mean at all anymore, came to my defense. He walked up to Kon, stood discourteously close, and said

134

to him, "Don't talk to her like that. Take it back, and be nice about it."

Jabe's slight advantage in height was enough to be menacing. He looked down at Kon, who had no choice but to look up, look down, or look away. Any option would have been a sign of defeat.

Kon took three steps back and looked at me with an enemy glare. "All right," he mumbled so no one could hear, "I take it back." Then he turned and vanished into the gathering crowd, looking for someone else to harass.

I liked having someone stand up for me.

"Thanks, Jabe," I said.

"Sure, Lin," he grinned.

"Why are they putting the tower on Mount Tantrill?" someone asked.

"Because it's closest to the sky," I said. "Closest to the satellite—"

And then, mid-sentence, it happened.

At first, only a few saw it. Their gasps of amazement — some close, some far — rolled across the crowd like a big wave spilling upon the shore. All eyes turned to the sky, and with the intensity of a thunder crash, the entire beach exploded in a deafening burst of joy and jubilation.

It was a sight never seen in Bree. A flying machine. It rose up over Mount Tantrill, coming gracefully into view — first the top, then the belly, then the underside. It was squat and round, silver-white, and ten times larger than the energy relay dish, which always looked so massive in size.

A second flying machine appeared close behind. Suspended from its body hung a tall, white tower. The sight of it made my hair stand on end. There she was, Bree's satellite receiving tower, our connection to the world, to the Continent, to culture, to outer space!

I jumped up on the Teaching Rock with Bissa's father's binoculars to get a good look.

"They're really here!" I cried. "Continentals!"

The first flying machine landed and four men walked out. The fact that they were really here was hitting me hard, making me shaky and dizzy and incapable of holding the binoculars steady to my eyes. I jumped off the Teaching Rock and gave the binoculars to Mira. A group of boys mauled her in a scramble to grab them from her hands.

"Animals," she complained after being thrown to the ground.

The binoculars were in such high demand that a spate of rank injustice broke out. The taller boys were snatching the binoculars from the shorter ones and not giving them back.

"We need to do something," I said to the Evolutionaries standing nearby. "There's not enough sharing going on."

"We need a system," Bissa said.

"Right," said Hali, "a system."

Mira held up her kipper-paper notebook. "I have an idea."

Mira's idea was simple but brilliant: make a list of everyone who wanted to use the binoculars and check them off when they had.

Word got out about Mira's list, and all through the morning, people of every age came to the Teaching Rock to catch a magnified view of the installation. Mira kept a flawless list, and Bissa stood close by to watchguard her father's prized binoculars. At the end of the day, 649 people had used them. When Bissa returned the binoculars to her father, to his great surprise, they had no scratches nor dents nor any other type of injury. He was so supremely pleased that he became one of our greatest supporters. "They're an impressive group of children," he would tell people. "Exemplars of maturity."

We called the incident the Binocular Sharing Program Invented on the Day They Installed the Satellite Tower. It was the first time we publicly demonstrated the values of love. We had found a way to fairly share a single object with a great number of people. At the next club meeting, "Share fairly" was adopted as one of our tenets.

The four men departed in their flying machines, leaving behind our new satellite receiving tower, which stood next to the energy relay dish like a long-lost companion. The crowd dispersed, most in search of lunch and dry cover. They had every reason to believe the job was done and there was no more left to see.

But there *was* more, and the lucky ones who weren't so quick to leave were treated to a second and even more thrilling event.

It happened without warning. We were gathered around the Teaching Rock where the waiting line for the binoculars was still 20 or 30 people long. A third flying machine approached Mount Tantrill, not from behind it as the others had that morning, but from behind *us*, from somewhere out at sea. Lo was the first to see it.

"Look!" she cried, pointing to the sky.

We turned and saw a smaller and fatter flying machine, hovering low above the sea and moving toward us at a medium clip. It carried a load, round in shape and dangling from a short rope. In the further distance, out on the Strellin Sea, we saw a boat, an odd boat, flat and long. On it sat two identical flying machines and the movement of people. Continentals, no doubt.

The Continentals

They were Continentals all right. I held the binoculars steady to my eyes and counted.

"One." *Thump*.... "Two." *Thump*.... "Three." *Thump*.... "Four." *Thump*.... I waited.

"Are there more?" someone asked.

"Don't know yet," I said.

"What are they doing?"

"Two walked back inside the flying machine."

"And the others?"

"They're walking over to the tower."

"And what about the load?"

"It's still sitting there."

It was just sitting there, the biggest, most mysterious wrapped package we'd ever seen, waiting to be opened, its mystery divulged.

I had counted four Continentals from my place high up on the Teaching Rock. For my schoolmates standing near, I counted with my loudest voice. For those standing far, I counted with a single, high-drawn tail thump that could be seen by everyone who still lingered on the beach.

"More are coming out of the flying machine!" I hollered.

"What are they doing?"

"Two are still inspecting the tower," I said. "Two are walking toward the package. The others are looking around on the ground."

"What are they looking for?"

"I don't think they're looking," I said, "I think they're measuring."

"Measuring what?"

"Not sure. But they're finally unwrapping the package."

"This is so exciting," Hali said.

"Tell us what's in the package when you see," said Bissa.

"You're going to know right now," I said. The Continentals had pulled a long rope that loosened the packaging, which fell to the ground, leaving a single object standing in simple glory. My jaw dropped. "Great sun above us," I said in disbelief.

"What?"

"What do you see?"

"It's a clarkon dome," I said, "a really big one that people can live in. I saw one on display at the Holograhic Library."

***

"They're going to live here?" someone asked as ten of us sat near the Teaching Rock to devour the lunches our mothers had packed in our satchels. Having no mother, Aunt Tala packed mine.

"Why *wouldn't* they live here?" said Hali. "They have work to do."

"Right," I said. "They have to stay somewhere while they finish the installation and teach us how to use our holophones."

We opened our lunches and waited for Bissa's call. How she became the leader and arbiter of our daily lunch routine, I don't remember. Maybe no one else wanted the responsibility.

Bissa raised her hand to get everyone's attention. "Food trade!" she yelled.

All talking, all nattering, all fidgeting stopped. Food trading was serious business.

"All right," Bissa said over the quiet, "who has snodfish today they'd like to trade?"

Six hands pointed skyward.

"Who *wants* snodfish and what do you have to trade for it?"

A girl named Mili spoke. "I have boiled turo bird."

"I'll take it!" said one of the six who didn't want their snodfish. He handed his sack of dried snodfish to the boy next to him, who passed it along until it reached Mili. Mili passed back her boiled turo bird.

Packed in my satchel was stufferfish, again, father's favorite fish. In the five months since mother's death, Aunt Tala had cooked so much stufferfish for father, I was sure he would have long grown tired of it. But he hadn't. As for me, I was so supremely tired of it, I would trade it for anything, even dried snodfish, which most people agreed tasted like salty wood.

"I have stufferfish," I said. I looked over at Hali, who was already offering me his snodfish, which his mother packed in his satchel with the same frequency as Aunt Tala packed stufferfish in mine. He loved stufferfish, and he and I had traded these two fishes so often this year, we probably set a new all-time record for the most trades of the same two foods.

When the food trade was over, we talked again of the Continentals, whose dome I could see from the place I chose to sit. It looked small without the binoculars, but even so, there was a majestic presence about it. Some may have thought it looked out of place here, since all the homes and buildings in Bree were made of wood and stone, but it looked quite fitting next to the energy relay dish and satellite receiving tower. I hoped the sight of them clustered together on top of Mount Tantrill would inspire the people of Bree to want to modernize and travel and take interest in culture and replace the Committee of No Technology with younger, progress-minded members.

"I wonder how long they'll stay," said a boy named Krin.

"Probably until the 21st or the day after," I told him.

"How would you know?" he asked.

"Didn't you read the silver paper?"

"Which part?"

"All of it," I told him. "There wasn't that much."

He shrugged. "Don't think I read it all. Or I could have forgot."

"They're giving out the holophones from the 15th to the 21st," I said. "After that, they're done."

"They came with 2,000 holophones," Bissa said. "One for anyone who wants one and then a bunch left over."

"What does it cost to get a holophone?" Rina asked.

"They're free," I said.

"Free?" asked Krin.

"How can they be free?"

"We can ask the Continentals when we see them," said Mira.

"I don't believe it," Krin said. "It must be a trick."

Bissa leaned forward. "What do you mean, a trick?"

Krin answered her with questions. "Two thousand holophones? They're giving to people they don't even know? For free?"

"Makes no sense," Chib mumbled.

"No sense," Krin agreed. "What do they get out of it? There has to be something."

"The joy of giving," I said.

Krin crinkled his face. "Since when is giving fun?"

"Right," said his cousin Chib.

I glared at them, my patience worn thin, and a burning anger rose without warning. You're turning into naysayers," I told them. "Right before my eyes!"

They only giggled.

"Lin's right," Bissa told them. "You're acting like adults, arguing over things you don't know anything about."

"This is the best day in the whole history of Bree," said Mira. "Where's your excitement and wonder?" She pointed up to Mount Tantrill. "Look! Have you ever seen anything more amazing than that? Don't you understand how it's going to change our lives forever? Life in Bree will never be the same."

Life in Bree never was the same.

"Did you hear it?" Aunt Tala asked me the next morning when I woke up.

"Hear what?"

"The emergency siren."

"No, what's wrong?"

"The Mayor's making an announcement."

I put a chunk of asi cake in my mouth, grabbed another, and ran outside.

A large crowd was already standing around the Sound Station when we arrived. Everyone was talking about the mysterious object that appeared overnight on top of Mount Tantrill. Some were curious, some were fearful, and some were panicked. Few adults knew what it was or where it came from. But Aunt Tala knew. I told her while we had made dinner the night before.

"It's all right," I said to my grandparents, who had already made their way to the Sound Station. "It's just the Continentals."

"It's temporary lodging," Aunt Tala told them.

"We should tell everyone," I said.

"No," Aunt Tala said, "let the Mayor do it."

"But—"

"No," she said.

I didn't insist. The lecture I got from her last week about being a well-intentioned menace was still fresh in my memory. "Your father says you're giving our family a bad name," she scolded. A bad name with the naysayers, I told her. Who cares what they think? "Your father cares," she said, "and we have to live with him. So tone it down, Lin. Try not to be so — so helpful and knowledgeable."

Mira agreed it was nutty advice from an adult to a child, but then again, it was true that life in my household followed no normalcy of any kind.

As we waited around the large catlin shell perched on top of an ancient tree stump at the Sound Station, I remembered what mother once told me when I asked her where the voice came from when town announcements were made, the voice that rather magically spoke from inside the catlin shell.

"A very long time ago," mother told me, "our ancestors invented a method of communicating important messages to the far ends of

Bree. They dug long, narrow trenches to different parts of town from a central point where the message would be spoken. In these trenches, they laid thousands and thousands of soni shells, one end fitted into the opening of another. They were very tightly stacked, end-to-end, and covered with dirt. This formed long, underground tubes made of soni shells."

"Why soni shells?" I asked her.

"They carry sound," mother said. "The whistle that the teachers wear is made of soni shells."

I smiled at my memory of mother, half happy, half sad. I wished she were here to see how Bree was modernizing. I imagined she was standing by my side, squeezing my hand, her face beautiful and smiling, her excitement as big as mine.

The crowd was restless, but few spoke. Huddled around the catlin shell, we waited. Some stared up at the clarkon dome and the new satellite tower, but most stared at the silent shell, waiting for the Mayor's words to spill out of it.

"Greetings, Breefolk," he finally said. "This is your Mayor."

Every voice stopped. All eyes were on the catlin shell, as if the Mayor himself were standing there. But I kept my eyes on the clarkon dome, hoping to catch a glimpse of our visitors, even though from here they would look no larger than a gri fly.

"There is no need to be alarmed," the Mayor said. "I repeat, there is no need to be alarmed. The structure you see on Mount Tantrill is the temporary lodging of eight men and women who are here throughout the week. Beginning tomorrow and every day until next Kodri, they will be stationed at the Pavillion from the 9th Hour to the 15th Hour, dispensing the holophone headpiece devices. I repeat...."

As the Mayor finished his announcement, I closed my eyes and thought about tomorrow, when the people of Bree would come face to face with the people of the Continent.

Slow, sleepy, backward little Bree was poised on the forward edge of a massive turning. A technological turning. We were about to turn a corner and find the whole world there — the whole world and more: the sun, the stars, our planetary neighbors, the entire universe!

We were about to be changed in a way none of us could really fully know — even me, the most progress-minded of us all.

THE SEAWALL OF NO

The next morning, big news awaited me. Good news and bad news — the crushing kind of bad.

In my ignorance, I happily walked to school with Mira.

"Did you sleep last night?" I asked her.

"Mmm," she hummed, "slept great."

"I hardly slept at all," I said, but not with complaint. "I couldn't stop thinking about today, the most everything-changing day Bree will ever know."

We passed by the last row of fishing quarters, a place where the footpath curved and descended toward East Bree Beach and the Teaching Rock. Here the splendor of Mount Tantrill came into view.

"Let's stop and look," I said.

"Sure," said Mira. "How about up here for a better view?"

We hopped up on a big flatrock and stared at the monuments of modernity that now graced Bree's only mountain.

"Hey, look," Mira said, "we're not the only ones."

I looked down at the beach and saw scattered groups of people staring up at Mount Tantrill — our schoolmates and older folks and even some fishermen.

"How can you not stop and stare?" I said. "It's so beautiful and inspiring. The whole world is ours now, Mira. The whole world!"

"And outer space," she rightly added. "And, you're right, Lin, it *is* beautiful. Even the energy relay dish looks good now. I never liked the sight of it, you know."

"I'm going to miss the clarkon dome when they take it away."

"Me too," said Mira. "I wonder what they're doing right this minute."

"I wonder too," I said. "They're not due at the Pavillion for another two hours."

"I think we should try to talk Teacher Hana into taking us there today."

I love-tugged Mira's good ear. "I was thinking exactly the same thing. Let's hurry and ask her before school starts."

No sooner had I said that than Teacher Hana's soni shell sounded three short whistles, the five-minute warning whistle. We laughed at the synchrony.

"Good sign," I said.

"Mere coincidence," Mira grinned.

We hopped off the flatrock and headed down to the Teaching Rock, rehearsing a strategy for convincing Teacher Hana in case she wasn't quick to approve our idea.

"No," she said when we made our request. "The Lower School classes are there today. We're going tomorrow."

Tomorrow. That was the good news.

The bad news destroyed it only minutes later.

"Now I've heard some of you talking," Teacher Hana said when we had all assembled for a lesson on rocks and where they came from, "and I don't want you to get your hopes up. Tomorrow is an instruction day *only*. You'll each be given a holophone to look at and learn with. But you won't be taking them home with you."

"We can't take them home?" I asked.

"You will," she said, "but not tomorrow. That will happen later, with your parents. All children need parental approval, in person, with a signature."

That was the bad news. I was going to have to fight for my holophone.

***

"Just when life gets good, it never fails to serve up some cruel injustice," I told Mira and Bissa on our way home from school.

"You more than most," said Mira.

"More than anyone I know," Bissa added with a rare sympathy.

Some of the injustices I had suffered were dealt by natural disasters, some by parental rules, some by parental moods, some by simple acts of stupidity or carelessness (a few of them mine), and some by baffling blows of undeserved bad luck. But this injustice was dealt by the Continentals themselves. This was their rule, not father's, and it was easily one of the top three cruelest injustices of my lifetime. Still, it didn't make me like them any less.

It was true that father's naysaying attitude was really to blame, but since he was responsible for more than half of my lifetime injustices, I decided not to blame him for this one.

That was before I saw him at dinner that night.

"Absolutely not!" he bellowed.

"Won't you at least come down and see them?" I asked.

"No," he said, "I have no interest in such things."

"But *I* have interest. Don't you care about that?"

"Ahhhh," was all he grumbled, which wasn't so bad. More often than not, grumbles signaled signs of a weakness somewhere in his Great Seawall of No. When father wouldn't answer a simple yes or no question with real words, I knew he could be turned.

I looked at Aunt Tala. She was going to be of no help at all. I could tell by that goofy smile and half-not-here look that she was daydreaming of Merchant Kam, who asked her just that morning to accompany him to the Nadri night dances. She thought he might be growing sweet on her and that made her happy. And when Aunt Tala was happy, she had no interest in tangling with father.

I was on my own on this one, though I knew Grandmother Min would have sided with me. Unlike father, she had interest in the world outside of Bree and wanted a holophone of her own. Even though she was older than father, she was a lot more progress-minded.

"Grandmother Min wants one," I said.

"Then you can use hers," father muttered.

"No," I told him, "actually I can't."

"Yes, you can. She lives just across the foyer, and she'll probably use it little."

"No, father, I *can't* use hers. And she couldn't use mine, if it were the other way around. You can't use another person's holophone because the headpiece you're given is programmed with your voice. It'll only recognize *your* voice."

"Then you can use hers without speaking," he stupidly said. "All the better to be quiet about it. Just don't talk when you're — when you're doing with it what you do."

"It doesn't work without talking," I said. "You have to *tell* it what to do. And it only recognizes *your* voice. The voice of the person the holophone belongs to."

He stared at me with the cold angry eyes of a grandis caught in a trapper's cage.

"There's no sharing solution," I said.

His eyes changed in an eerie transfiguration, from squint-slit angry eyes to wide-open furious eyes. "There's no *sharing solution*?" he shouted. "Where are you getting these words?"

"They're just words, Jorn," Aunt Tala said. "Simple words even you know. If you haven't noticed by now, Lin has a good intelligence for language. You should be proud of the fact. I am."

Aunt Tala love-tugged my ear and smiled at me as would a mother who loved her daughter more than anything else in the world. I liked Aunt Tala happy, even if that meant she wouldn't fight father on my behalf.

"Of all the children in Bree," I said to father, "I'm the most deserving. *I'm* the one who brought satellite broadcast reception to Bree in the first place. Without my petition—"

"Ah, ah, ah," he said with a wave of his finger. "You know that's a forbidden word."

I couldn't make the petition defense. Petition was still forbidden.

148

"Aunt Tala," I asked, "you're getting a holophone, aren't you?"

"Of course," she said, "I want to see the views of space and listen to the broadcasts on business and trade."

"There," father said, "you two can share."

"Father, we *can't* share," I moaned. "Are you *really* going to deprive me of this? Can't you see how supremely important this is to me? How unhappy and permanently damaged I'll be if you deprive me of a holophone, which everyone in Bree except the naysayers will have? I know you're the parent and get to make the rules, but you have to remember what it was like when you were the kid and Grandmother Min and Grandfather Daun were making rules that you had to obey. Weren't some of them unusually cruel and unjust?"

Aunt Tala let out a laugh, and I could tell by the frown of father's mouth that he had to force himself from smiling.

"I remember how much you hated lightning curfew," she said.

"Lightning curfew?" I asked.

"Your father loved watching the lightning shows down at the pier. Mother wouldn't let him."

"How old was he?"

"Oh, about your age. Remember, Jorn?"

Father nodded, and a small smile began to show. "I remember," he said. "She forbid me from going to the piers after dark."

"She though it was too dangerous," Aunt Tala told me. "But your father went anyway. He would sneak out his sleepingroom window when they slept. And for the longest time, he got away with it. But mother finally found out, and then she made all lightning shows forbidden. Even during the day."

"That's cruel," I said. "Don't you think, Aunt Tala? Pretty cruel."

"I'd say so."

Father remained quiet, his mood hidden.

"Did you still sneak down to the pier?" I asked him.

"I never went to the pier," he said, soft and proud, "they knew to look for me there. I went up to the cave dwellings where I knew they couldn't find me."

"And you watched the lightning shows from there?"

"Yes," he said and closed his eyes. "Yes," he said again, smiling at what seemed a happy, far-away memory.

"What, father?" I asked.

He opened his moist eyes. Whatever it was, it had brought forth his inner sanctum of sweetness. I saw it in his eyes, and I knew it by what he said next.

"I first kissed a girl there," he said, "watching a lightning show in the early evening. I was seventeen."

"Who was she?" I asked.

"Mora ji Bel," he and Aunt Tala said in one voice. Aunt Tala laughed at the joy of it, and father did too.

"But you didn't marry her," I said.

"Your father didn't marry a lot of girls," Aunt Tala said. "All the girls found him quite handsome. He had one girlfriend after another before he met your mother."

"That's a far stretch, Tala," he said.

"I'd say you had six girlfriends over the years," she told him.

"Do you ever see these old girlfriends?" I asked father.

"Some of them."

"Really? Here in Bree?"

He nodded and inhaled his last kriddle cake. I imagined him as a teenager, strapping and handsome and rule-breaking.

"I like it that you snuck up to the cave dwellings to watch the lightning shows," I said.

"When I was your age," Aunt Tala said. "I wasn't allowed to go to the marketplace alone. But I went anyway, on days I knew, or thought I knew, that mother wouldn't be there. But I forgot to think about the fact that her friends might see me there and mention it to her."

"Did that ever happen?" I asked.

"Yes."

"Did you get in big trouble?"

"Pretty big. It seemed so at the time, anyway."

"It's no fun to sneak around the rules of our parents," I said. "The fear of being caught can take all the fun out of what you're doing."

"Oh," father said, "and what things are you doing that you're afraid of being caught for?"

"Nothing these days, father. Nothing. But I will say this," since his mood now was good, "I know I could figure out a sneaky way to get my own holophone and never tell you and only use it when you're not around. But I won't do it. It wouldn't be fun, and it wouldn't be right. I'm the leader of the Evolutionaries Club, and I have a duty to be a good person, even in secret. So if I want something supremely badly, I have to get it the right way, not the sneaky way."

"You have a duty to be good," father said. He nodded and leaned back in his chair. He seemed pleased with me. "A leader has many duties," he said, "and one of them is to be a good example to those he leads. That's good, Lin, it's good that you understand this."

"Thanks, father. I want so much to make you proud of me."

"I *am* proud of you. You're not afraid to take action."

There was my opening.

"Father," I said, "will you reconsider? Will you agree to let me have my own holophone?"

He said nothing. My insides turned and twisted with creeping excitement, anticipating his agreement.

"I truly believe I'm mature enough," I said. "And I'm getting more mature all the time."

Father broke a smile. "That was funny, Lin. You're getting more mature all the time." He squinted at me as if to see something the eyes don't ordinarily see. "You are," he said. "You are."

Aunt Tala seized the moment. "Jorn, I think she should have one. I know you have mixed feelings about it, but she pulled off an amazing feat. She did that, Jorn, through her own willfulness and courage and tenacity. She's a lot like you, you know. Your better qualities."

Father stretched his neck, first to the left and then to the right, which always meant one wonderful thing — a change of mind. "I don't agree with it," he said, "and I don't believe in it, but that doesn't change the fact that you deserve it, Lin." He drew in a long breath while my belly somersaulted. "So," he nodded, "I'll sign the paper."

"Father!" I cried.

I leapt up, ran to his side of the table, and hugged him from behind. "Thank you, father! You won't regret this, I'm sure of it."

"All right, all right, all right," he said as he patted my head with his large, heavy hand.

"I love you, father," I whispered in his ear.

"I love you, too, Lin. Now finish your dinner, you've hardly eaten. And Lin?"

"Yes, father?"

"No thumping."

I stopped thumping and sat down to finish my kriddle fishcakes.

THE GIRL WITH THE WHITE EYES

One look at her, and we were mesmerized.

She stood alone at a flatrock table, waiting for us with bright smile. We were told her name was Ki. We liked her instantly and nicknamed her the Girl With the White Eyes, even though, technically, they weren't white but a very light blue.

"What's wrong with your eyes?" one of my schoolmates asked her.

She laughed and said, "Although your question was not politely asked, I understand its intent." She spoke Welbi as well as the translators at the Embassy Island. "You may know that there are many variations in eye color among Luratians. Here in Southern Wershonia your eyes are orange, yellow, and green. Where I come from, our eyes are violet and blue."

While my schoolmates and Teacher Hana fell into a Ki-trance, I eyed the four boxes on the flatrock table. One was much larger than the others. *There they are,* I thought. My tail thumped, my hair stood on end, and my mind raced with holographic anticipation.

"Why are you giving these to us for free?" Krin couldn't wait to ask.

"These were made a long time ago and most people no longer use them," Ki said. "Instead of being thrown away, they are given away."

"They're throw-away phones," I whispered to Bissa.

"Guess so," she said.

"Now," said Ki, "are you ready to learn about holophones?"

We shouted that we were.

"Holophones are programmed for one person only," Ki explained. "They power-on by reading the color and pattern of your eyes. This means that no one can power-on your holophone but you. You may not care much about that now, but as you get older, you will appreciate this security feature. When you first receive your holophone, it takes a picture of your eyes and holds that picture in memory as the correct power-on eyes. The same is true for your voice. If you are wearing your holophone and a mischievous friend comes along and speaks a command into it, nothing will happen."

Ki reached inside the biggest of the boxes, pulled out a holophone, and held it high for everyone to see.

"This," she said, "is a holophone."

"Oooo," my schoolmates hummed, stunned by its unusualness.

It was a clear-colored cap with two holes for the ears to stick through and an invisible clarkon screen that covered the eyes.

"These are special holophones and are not yours to keep," Ki said before she and Teacher Hana made the rounds, positioning a holophone on each of our heads. "You will pick up your own later with your parents. These holophones are programmed to read any eyes and any voice speaking the Welbi language. They won't power-on until everyone has one, so be patient and don't be concerned that nothing is happening yet."

It was Teacher Hana who fitted me.

"Feel this," she said.

She put the holophone in my hands, and we laughed.

"It's so squishy," she laughed like a child. "It feels like a gelfish, smooth and slimy!"

She was right. A holophone did feel like a squishy gelfish. The only solid part was the slightly curved, rectangular screenpiece that covered the eyes. The rest of it bended and folded like a piece of fabric. I wadded it up in my hands and let go. It stretched out fully to its permanent shape. Teacher Hana and I laughed and laughed as we watched it jiggle.

"I'm happy for this day," she said.

"I'm crazy happy," I told her. "Father agreed last night to let me have my own holophone. He was against it at first."

"You did some good convincing?"

"Yes, and it wasn't too excruciating, not like I thought."

"I'm glad to know that, Lin." She positioned the holophone on my head and pulled my ears through the holes. "Now, how does that feel?"

"Like there's hardly anything there."

"They're surprisingly lightweight, aren't they?"

I nodded. "It's the clarkon, you know. Clarkon in Bree, can you believe it?"

"I suppose I wouldn't have, but I do now."

The screenpiece was solid but completely clear as if not there at all, just like the clarkon sidewall of the boat I rode to the Embassy Island. The cap was clear enough to see one's hair underneath. I looked around at my schoolmates. From even a small distance, I could hardly see their holophones. From a greater distance, if someone was wearing a holophone, you wouldn't even know it.

"Lin!" It was Mira.

"I'm over here!" I waved until she saw me.

She hopped over, laughing with a joy I'd never seen in her, her bent ear flopping. *I really need to tell her not to hop in public,* I reminded myself.

"Look!" Mira tapped on her screenpiece. "It looks like there's nothing there," she tapped again, "but there is!"

"Yes!" we shouted.

"All right, I'm activating them to power-on."

Our holophones made a short but beautiful sound. Were it the sound of a bird, it would be coveted as a pet.

"All right," Ki said, "we're going to begin with an experience of simulated flight. We do this by engaging the Flight Mode. And we do this by saying, 'Command ... Flight Mode'. Now let's say it together."

"Command ... Flight Mode," we said.

The screenpiece turned from clear to black, and there we stood, like it were the dark of night.

"As you can see," Ki said, "the screenpiece can be clear or dark like it is now or anywhere in between. When the screenpiece is so dark that moving around would be dangerous, your holophone will automatically power-off if you move any distance. So during this experience, stay where you're standing, or your holophone will power-off."

Blissfully blind, we laughed, curious and motionless, ready for an adventure of certain magnificence.

"Now that you're in Flight Mode," Ki said, "you need to give it a voice command or else you'll go nowhere. The command is simple. You say where you're leaving from and where you're going to. Listen to me first, and when I tell you to, repeat what I say…. Depart Strellin Embassy, arrive Mount Tantrill…. Now, all together."

We said words, and in the blackness appeared the sea. It looked so real, I feared I'd fall in. Since mother's death, I was terrified of the sea. Swimming used to be my favorite thing, but now I avoided it, certain I'd never swim again. And here I was, hovering over a vast, choppy sea, held up by nothing. The feeling was frightening, but exhilarating too. Beneath my fear, I knew I was safe.

Then, the incredible happened.

What we saw was more than a picture. It was more than a moving picture. It was movement itself. We were *flying*, soaring through the air like a seabird, flying low over the sea. The feeling of flying was so real, I felt my body rise and dip, I felt wind in my hair, I tasted the sea mist, I got dizzy flutters when I rose higher in the sky. I felt not at all like me but like a seabird. I was flying! Flying! Flying and laughing and wanting it never to end.

"Soon you will see the beaches of Southern Wershonia," we heard Ki say. "The large beaches to the west of Bree."

There it was, a beach! We turned sharply, dove downward, and flew along the coastline. We passed over a watertaxi, then a fleet of fishing boats, then a village. We passed more villages, then a town, then a large city with tall buildings not anything like the buildings of Bree. We passed over a stretch of empty beach, then a small village, then a town, and then another city, bigger than the first.

Instinctively, I turned my head to see more of the city. I saw tight clusters of buildings, some tall and skinny, some squat and fat, some completely round like a ball. In the distance were sprawling spaces filled with dome-topped homes and high-fenced fields and monorail tracks that disappeared into the far horizon. We rose up over a hill that had a big hole in the top. I had seen it before in a picture book of volcanoes and cried at the joy of recognizing it. I knew where we were now. Soon we would pass over Kuli, north of which was Vola's town of Donnot.

When we reached Kuli, I looked to the North. Small and medium towns dotted the land as far as I could see. One of those medium towns was Vola's, I wished I knew which. I waved to her anyway.

We passed along the route the watertaxi takes from Kuli to Bree. Soon we would be here. The thought of it was funny, flying over ourselves. Two places at once. A seabird in the air and a person on the ground.

"And here is Bree," said Ki.

"There's Hallo's Farm!" someone cried.

"I see the mosswoods!" said another.

"My house!" Hali shouted. "I can see my house!"

We flew over Bissa's house, Mira's house, the marketplace, and the Big Orange.

"There's the Pavillion!"

"There we are!"

We shouted as we flew low over the Pavillion, over the fishing quarters where I lived, and up over the cave dwellings to the top of Mount Tantrill, where we circled around the energy relay dish, the new satellite tower, and the clarkon dome where Ki slept at night. We landed near the cliff's edge and looked down on Bree Beach. Slowly, our view dimmed and blackened.

The blackness vanished, and there we stood, in Bree Pavillion, which we had never left on our voyage through the sky.

"Can we do that again?" someone asked.

"I want to see Egli!" hollered someone else.

"Yeah, Egli!"

"There is so much more to show you," Ki said. "So, no, that's all the low-sky flying we'll do for now. But I'm confident you won't be disappointed with where we go next."

"Where are we going?" she was asked.

"Many places," she said. "Outer space, for one."

Ki was right, we weren't disappointed. We traveled up the space elevator to the Forton satellite, passing clear through the clouds and into the sunshine on the other side. We passed through our atmosphere into the jeweled blackness of space. So many stars! Some of them, Ki said, were homes to worlds like ours. We sailed past the planets in our solar system. We roamed outer space and saw up close the beautiful double star Albereo, made of a golden yellow star and small blue star that will constantly spin around each other — "locked in orbital embrace," Ki said, "for 10 billion years."

I learned that day that our holophones could give us every amazing experience we could get at the World Library. Now we didn't need to take the trouble to actually go there, and even better, we wouldn't have to petition the School Board to get permission for it. It was a petition I knew would have been monumentally controversial. Now it was a fight we didn't have to fight.

And this came as a great relief. I had another fight to fight. A personal one. It would be the biggest, toughest, longest fight of my life, the one I cared most about.

CALLING VOLA

Their work was done and they had gone.

The Continentals left as they came, except in reverse: They collapsed and bundled their clarkon dome, tied it to their flying machine, and flew out to sea.

"Though to be more precise," Mira wrote in her kipper-paper notebook, "the clarkon dome collapsed and bundled *itself*." How, we did not know.

Teacher Hana didn't try to teach us anything that day, the day the Continentals left. Standing quietly, as if at a funeral, she and my schoolmates watched them disappear into the low-hanging clouds that blanketed the Strellin Sea. Fighting back tears, I turned away from the sea and looked up at Mount Tantrill.

"You're sad," Mira whispered.

"A little," I said. "There's a bald spot now on Mount Tantrill that'll be painful to look at."

"Why don't you look instead at what they left behind?" she said in a moment of brilliance.

"You're right, Mira," I said.

Don't be sad about what's missing, I thought, *be happy for what you have.* I figured that would be a good attitude for how to live life, which is always taking away from you, sometimes the things you most want to keep. But life, I knew, wouldn't take everything away. Some precious things would never be taken and new precious things would always come. Eventually.

"Hey," I said, "want to call each other?"

"Sure," Mira said.

Mira and I had spoken to each other three times already that day, and the idea of another was no less exciting.

"Who's calling who?" Mira asked.

"You call me."

We powered-on our holophones and walked in opposite directions.

"Remember," she said, "how worried I've been about how we're going learn Culti since no one in Bree speaks it?"

I nodded a nod that she could see, though she was a good twenty paces behind me.

"I've been doubting it will ever happen," I said. "Merchant Kam's the only one who knows Culti, and he's way too busy and important to teach it to the rest of us."

"Well, I found a solution," Mira beamed. "The Education Broadcasts have Culti lessons."

"We can learn Culti on our holophones?"

"Yes," she said, "now we don't need to import teachers."

"Mira, that's great news! Now people will see how helpful holophones can be!"

"I'm so relieved," she said.

I was too. Mira and I and her father were convinced that no Culti-speaking teachers who also spoke Welbi would want to come to Bree and stay long enough to teach an entire village. Not unless they were handsomely paid. Mira's father said that Bree could never afford it. Learning Culti was going to be a big problem.

"Holophones are the best thing that ever happened to Bree," I said.

Mira smiled and nodded. "I wonder how many other problems they're going to solve for us."

"I think we've only seen a single strand of the trissilfish nest."

"Your dream came true, Lin. You brought clarkon and progress to Bree. Big progress."

"Makes me almost not want to leave. But...."

160

"But what?"

"But I will. I have to. I want to."

"I won't miss you so much now," Mira said.

"Isn't that the best? We can talk anytime."

"And see each other."

"And I can show you where I live and what I'm doing," I said.

"I saw that you turned."

"And I can see that you're sitting on the pier."

We laughed and laughed, though nothing funny was said.

"Life will never be the same, Mira."

"Want to look at more stuff from the World Library?" she asked.

"I can't. It's the day I'm calling Vola."

"Oh." I could see Mira's disappointment.

"This willl be our first call," I told her. "Next time we talk, I want to introduce you to her."

"You will?"

"Yes," I said, "she really wants to meet you. She's a fan of your writing. She read your article in *The Strellin National Recorder*."

"I like her already," Mira said.

We laughed again, love-tugged our own ears, and said goodbye.

***

I had decided that morning that the cave dwellings would be the best place to be when I called Vola. From there I could show her Bree Beach, the piers and fishing boats, the Teaching Rock and lightning shelter, part of the marketplace, and our corner of the fishing quarters.

"And do you see that wood building?" I told Vola early in our call. She was as eager to see Bree as I was to show her. "The one you can only partly see?"

"Yes," she said, "I see it."

"That's where I live. Those are the fishing quarters where the fishermen and their families live."

"You're so close to the water," she said, her eyes wide with envy or wonder or both.

"I can hear the waves at night," I told her. "They help me fall asleep. If I ever lived away from the sea, I wonder if I'd sleep at all."

"You could get a sound-making machine," Vola said, "one that makes the sound of the sea."

"A machine? That makes sound?"

She nodded. "Father has one that makes the sound of birds."

"I guess people are happy with the sounds we have. I've never heard anyone talk of wanting a sound machine."

"That's strange. Everyone here wants sounds. You know, pretty ones or wild ones or soothing ones, depending on your mood. That's why you can find so many different kinds on your holophone."

"Where do I find these sounds?" I asked.

"From the World Portal, say 'Sound Library'."

"I never thought I would talk to a machine."

"There's something else you should know about," Vola told me.

"What's that?"

"The portal for the International Schools."

I shivered, eartip to tailtip. "They have their own portal?"

"They do," Vola smiled. "I go there all the time. It has everything you need to know about the schools. Applying and the curriculum and the teachers. There are pictures of the campuses too."

"How do I get there?"

"From the World Portal, say 'International Schools'. Then you'll see lots of words on the screen that will show you different things. Just say which one."

"I can see them all I if I want," I said.

"Whenever you want."

We laughed, and seeing each other laugh, we laughed more.

"When are you going to apply?" Vola asked.

"When I talk my father into it."

"How much is he against it?"

"I think he's more against this than anything I'll ever ask for."

"That bad?"

"Yes," I said. "But I'm confident. He was supremely against the petition, and look what happened. You can't see the satellite tower from here, but next time we talk, I'll stand on the Teaching Rock and show it to you."

"I've never seen such a simple place as Bree."

"That's a nice way of putting it."

"It can't really be as backward as you say."

"Believe me, Vola, it is. We're a half step up from Egli on the evolutionary scale."

Vola laughed. "So, how are the naysayers taking all this?"

"They're out of their minds," I said, "complaining about how much everyone's using their holophones. They're calling it a mass holophone obsession, which I suppose it is, but what'd they expect?"

"It'll die down in a while."

"I think you're right," I said, certain and relieved that the naysayers would soon stop their fussing. "You know what's strange about the naysayers? They seem to *like* their naysaying."

"How do you mean?"

"You would think they'd be angry, especially now that the petition passed and the Continentals came and the tower's up and everyone — nearly — has a holophone. Everything the naysayers were against has happened. But they seem happier, not angrier. Not *happy* happy. It's an odd kind of happiness. I asked Teacher Hana about it, and she said that some people are naturally contrary and like having something to fight against."

"My great-grandmother's a naysayer," Vola said. "She doesn't like anything. You can serve her the most delicious kineberry pie, and she'll find fault with it. And you're right, she seems to enjoy it."

"Makes me think the naysayers might never stop complaining about the holophones. But they'll stop eventually, right? They have to."

"They have to," Vola agreed. "And what about your father?"

"Barely tolerating it. He doesn't want a holophone, but he's gotten curious. I saw him watching Aunt Tala when she was talking to Merchant Kam in the kitchen this morning."

"I hope he agrees to let you apply," Vola said.

"Yeah, well, it might take forever," I said, tired of the topic. "You're not outside. Are you in your house?"

"This is my sleepingroom."

"You have so many books," I said, eyeing a circular book shelf that had more books stacked on it than our entire school library.

"Some I've had for a long, long time," she said. "They're only suitable for kids now. But I'm saving them for my own children."

Her own children. Yes, she would have them someday. And I, too, would be a mother. I wondered what I had to give to my someday children.

"These," she said, spinning three rows of books in the center of the stack, "are my schoolbooks for Lower School. And these," pointing to the top of the stack, "are my favorite books."

"What are they about, your favorite books?"

"History mostly. I have five books on the history of Artunne, you know, the Continent. My favorite is called *The Flowering of Artunne*. It's written like a long story. It tells how the Continent became the Continent."

A pang of envy pinched me. I had never thought that such a book existed, but of course it would in more modern places. Our schools only had history books of Wershonia.

"It's strange to be here in Bree and there in Donnot," I said, "both at the same time. I feel like I'm standing in your house, standing right in front of you."

"It's one of the most great things about holophones," Vola said, "traveling without going anywhere. I like being in Bree. I've never been in a cave before."

"Our ancestors lived in these caves. Some were made by the water and wind, and some caves were carved by hand. You can still see some of the stone marks."

"Your town is so different from mine," Vola said. "You've lived such a different life."

"Hey, when you meet Mira," I thought to say, "there's something I should tell you."

"What?"

"One of her ears is bent."

"A lot?"

"Enough to notice."

"Oh, poor girl."

"I know. Sometimes I wonder which is worse, being a girl with a bent ear or a man with a missing leg."

"A man with a missing leg?"

"My father," I said. "I'll tell you about it sometime."

"Is he all right with it?"

"Not really."

"How does he walk?"

"With a wooden leg."

"Does it hurt?"

"I think so. I know in the beginning, when it happened, it hurt a lot."

"I can't imagine being without a leg or having a bent ear," Vola said. "Though there's an operation for that, you know."

"For bent ears?"

"Yes, there's a name for it I can't remember. My mother works at the hospital. I'll ask her about it."

"Your mother's a nurse?" I asked.

"An administrator. She's the boss of the nurses. What does your mother do?"

My heart collapsed and my breathing stopped. I didn't know what to say. I wasn't ready to tell Vola about mother. But I wasn't going to lie, either.

"Are you all right?" Vola asked.

"I'm all right," I said, waving my hand as if to brush something away, "just sidetracked by a memory." I smiled. "A Lower School

Teacher, my mother. Three years ago she won the Most Gently Effective Disciplinarian Competition at school. My father was so proud. I'll tell you all about her sometime."

"Speaking of competitions," Vola said.

And that was that, I made it through the awkwardness. We made no further mention of mother in our conversation. We talked about competitions, the International Schools, learning Culti, and the fact that on the North and South Poles the cloud layers are so thin that patches of pure sky can be seen for days at a time.

"That's why space exploration was invented on the North Pole," Vola said. "There's a huge space center there. You should go sometime."

I walked happily home, eager to tell Aunt Tala about the North Pole and its pure skies.

"Did you know that the sun shines on the North and South Poles?" I told her while we made dinner. "For days on end, skies of sunshine."

Aunt Tala was preoccupied. "Days on end?" she asked with mild enthusiasm.

And then we heard it.

My Life, Ruined

Slide, thud. Slide, thud. Slide, thud. The footsteps were father's.

"I hope he's not angry," I said.

Aunt Tala gutted another snodfish. "With your father," she said, "you never know."

"I feel sad for father, the older I get."

"That's good, Lin. He needs compassion."

Slide, thud. Slide, thud. Slide, slide, thud.

"He's reached the stairs," I said.

"All right, act normal."

"How about happy?"

"I don't know, Lin."

"I could tell him about the pure skies or the Clarkon Flats."

"No," she said, "too risky."

"Do you have any good news to tell him?"

"I have news, but I don't know if he'd find it good."

"Oooooo! What news?"

The front door opened.

"Later," she whispered.

"Hello, father!" I loudly said. "We're grilling snodfish!"

Father slid around the corner, lifted off his satchel, and dropped it to the floor, where it remained until the next morning when Aunt Tala filled it with sacks of food for his midday meal.

"Good," he said. "I'm as hungry as a grandis in the Egli desert."

"Well, I hope there's enough, Jorn."

"I can make some extra kriddlecakes," I said.

Father smiled. He always liked kriddlecakes, and since I'd been cooking with Aunt Tala, he liked mine best. "That'd be fine, Lin."

"How about some tichi tea and kono?" Aunt Tala asked.

"That'd be fine too. Will you bring it to me?"

"I'd be glad to," she said.

Father squinted at her for a long moment, as if there was more to say, but he said nothing until he turned and walked away. "Have to get off my leg," he muttered.

As she readied his tea, Aunt Tala's true mood shown forth. She was happy about something.

"Is his door shut?" I asked when she returned from delivering his tea and kono.

"Yes," she smiled. "Even so, let's keep our voices down."

"What's the news?"

"Merchant Kam is traveling to Orilon next month on an important business trip. He wants me to go with him."

"Orilon?!" I whispered the scream. "That's the most modern country in Wershonia! Did you say yes?"

"Of course I did."

"What about father?"

"He's not my parent."

"I guess you're right," I said. "You seem supremely happy about it, and I'm happy for you. Guess you really need to learn Culti now."

Aunt Tala laughed. "I'll learn it as fast as I can, but Kam's bi-lingual, so he can translate for me."

"You called him Kam."

"What?"

"You called him Kam, not Merchant Kam."

"Well, we work together," she said. "It's easier that way."

"Tala and Kam, that sounds nice." Aunt Tala laughed and swatted me with a diningcloth. "Tala and Kam, Tala and Kam, Tala and Kam." I laughed and laughed, but not too loud.

"Have you even started on those kriddlecakes?" she asked.

"I'm just about to put in the turo eggs. I beat them to a frenzy first. That's my secret for making—" *Tip, tap. Tip, tap.* "Hey! Do you hear?"

We trained our ears to the half-open window and listened. The footsteps stopped at the base of our front steps then began again. *Tip, tap. Tip, tap,* up the steps.

"Someone's here," I whispered.

Aunt Tala looked out the window. "It's him."

"Who?"

"Kam."

***

The commotion was mild, as far commotions go. Father didn't like being disturbed by Aunt Tala's emergency announcement that she was going for an important business dinner with Merchant Kam. He doubly didn't like that she asked him to be polite and greet Merchant Kam before they left.

"Tell him I'm incapacitated from an injury," Merchant Kam and I heard father say from where we stood in the kitchen. I suppressed a laugh, but not completely. Merchant Kam looked down at me and smiled. He gestured toward the front door, took my arm, and led us there.

"They need to have their privacy," he said when we were out of hearing range.

Alone now with Merchant Kam, my mind filled with a krillion questions, but I remembered what Aunt Tala said about letting *him* ask the questions, so I only said, "It's nice to see you again, Merchant Kam."

"It's a delight to see you, Lin. How are you taking to your holophone?"

"I don't know how I ever lived without it. Today I flew over the Clarkon Flats. Did you know the sun shines on the North and South Poles?"

"Yes, the best pure sky conditions in all the world are at the poles."

"And the worst are here," I said.

"Unfortunately, yes. That's because we're so near the equator."

"Oh."

"What else have you discovered of interest on your holophone?" he asked.

"The International Schools Portal. I want to apply."

Merchant Kam's eyes widened, big and bright, one then the other. "The International Schools ... I know them well," he softly spoke. "I was a student there myself."

A burst of joy exploded in me. "You've gone to the schools?"

"Yes. And I heartily recommend it. You're a perfect candidate, in fact."

"You think so?"

"Are you the founder and leader of the Evolutionaries Club?"

"Yes."

"That's all I need to say."

He gently love-tugged my ear, and I giggled.

Slide, thud. Slide, thud. Slide, thud. Here came father.

"Well, hello, Mr. di Ana," Merchant Kam said as he bowed his head the smallest bit.

"Hello," father said. "I hear you have a business dinner with my sister, and a picnic at that."

"Yes, were it not an urgent matter, I would suggest we all enjoy a picnic dinner on my boat," said Merchant Kam. "We'll have to do it another time."

Father cleared his throat. "Another time, yes."

Merchant Kam smiled. "Your daughter was telling me of her interest in the International Schools," he said.

I screamed inside — *No!!*

Father looked at me with grandis-angry eyes. Then he looked at Merchant Kam, smiling as he said, "She was, was she?"

I looked at the floor, horrified and drowning in dread. *No, no, no*

... this isn't happening ... this isn't happening ... this can't be happening....

I closed my eyes to shut out this excruciating moment. In the darkness, I saw my hope crumbling into a krillion pieces, into sand, into dust, then blown to the far reaches of space. One sentence, innocently spoken, forever ruined my plan for finding the perfect moment to talk to father about applying to the Schools.

"I'm a graduate myself," said Merchant Kam, oblivious to the damage he'd done. "It's a magnificent life education. I think Lin would excel there and be greatly edified by the experience."

Merchant Kam was ruining my life with his helpful words, and there was nothing I could do about it. I desperately wanted to put all the words back in his mouth and make him talk about anything but the Schools. I looked at Aunt Tala and she at me, ashen and sympathetic. My heart burned with a pain I hadn't felt since the day mother slipped from my arms and drowned in the sea. I stared at the floor and said nothing. *My life is ruined.*

"I see," father said, cold like ice.

I felt him staring at me, but I couldn't lift my eyes from the floor.

"Well," said Merchant Kam, cheerful and oblivious to the damage he'd done, "we'll leave you two to your evening."

As we said our goodbyes, Aunt Tala love-tugged my ear with the sweetest sweetness I'd ever felt from her. "Don't go," I wanted to say. "Please don't go."

"Goodbye," I said instead as father pulled the door shut.

The hard, heavy sound sealed my imprisonment. I was alone with him now. Alone to deal with a monumental mess.

Father stood silently at the door, and I stood silently behind him, frozen in fear. I was already walking too close to the edge of the pier, as father liked to say. Was this the one step that would cause me to fall?

And if I fell, I wouldn't fall into the swimmable sea, I would fall into a deep abyss of NO. That's how close I felt to being forever banned from the International Schools.

"Let's eat," father finally said. He turned and walked past me, taking his seat at the dining table.

I drew a deep breath and thought of mother. *I wish you were here, mother.* Life with father was so difficult without her.

A tear fell to the floor. I turned, careful not to step on it, and made my way to the kitchen.

THE GRANGE BELLY

I served our snodfish and kriddlecakes in silence and sat across from father, terrified to look at him and lacking any appetite. I forced myself to eat so he wouldn't have reason to be more angry at me than he already was.

Father devoured two snodfish, silent and famished, then finally said, "If you think you're going to those schools, you have sorely misunderstood me. You're not going, Lin."

Since he wasn't hollering, I decided to be bold and truthful.

"It won't do any harm just to apply," I told him. "If I'm accepted, they won't force me to go. You can say no, and I won't go. I just want to apply. I want to know if they would accept me into their schools."

"Isn't there a cost to apply?"

"No."

"Tala said you have to travel to the Embassy to apply. There's cost in that."

"Just a watertaxi for the three of us," I said.

"You and Tala and ... *me?*"

"Yes, you're both required to be there." I choked on the words. They were words I wanted not to say.

Father smiled. I crumpled. I knew what he was thinking. He found his rock solid line of defense. He would refuse to go to the Embassy Island to interview with the Admission Committee. And if he didn't go with me, my application would be incomplete and nullified.

"I'm not going to the Embassy," he said. "And that's final."

"You heard, father, how much Aunt Tala liked going. She—"

"I heard and heard. I've heard enough, too much. Too much for the length of my lifetime. The greatest peace I shall know is never to hear another word about the Continentals, their technology, their school, their Embassy, and I sure as thunder don't want to *go* there."

"But father—"

"And I don't want *you* to go, either."

"Of everything I've ever asked—"

"Not to the Embassy, not to the school."

"This means—"

"No.

"This means more to me—"

"No!"

"But father—"

"No means no!"

"Don't be cruel!" I yelled.

Father's eyes turned a terrifying shape of angry — thin-slit vicious eyes, the eyes of a noxi lizard staring down his prey. He pounded his fist on the table, swift and sudden. It took me unexpected, and I jumped — more from surprise than from fear.

"Don't play frightened, Lin. It won't work. I know your tricks."

"I wasn't. I was just surpri—"

"And don't you *dare* accuse me of cruelty! I work to the point of pain every day to feed you! I've given you everything you've asked for. I agreed to your holophone, against my better judgment. I allow you your subversive club activities. I defend you when people speak ill of you!"

Subversive? It was a word I didn't know. If I had my holophone, I could have looked up its meaning in an instant. Where did father get that word, anyway? I'd never heard him say it before and usually if a big word was spoken around here, father was the last to know its meaning. *His naysayer friends gave him that word.* That's what I thought.

"Cruel?" father shouted. "Most tell me I'm too lenient with you! Well, that's stopping now. It's time to rein you in. You're a danger to yourself, to us, to Bree. You disgrace our family name. Do you have any idea what you put me through every single day? Some of the fish merchants won't buy my fish because of you!"

"Because of me? I'm just a girl."

"Is that what you think?"

"Yes!"

"An innocent little girl?"

What was he getting at? "Yes, father, I'm just a girl! What's wrong with that?"

"You really don't get it, Lin."

"Get what?"

"You're bringing Bree to ruin!" father hollered.

I hollered back. "Bringing Bree to ruin? I'm helping!"

"Well, most folks don't *like* your kind of helping."

"Most folks want to modernize Bree. Not like the North, but at least a little. Don't you see how much we've been missing out on? There's a whole fascinating world out—"

"We don't want the world!" father bellowed.

"Who? Who doesn't want the world?"

"More than I can name."

"But not everyone."

"You don't hear what I hear," father said. "They say you're a revolutionary who's going to destroy our way of life with your childish flights of fancy."

"I'm not a revolutionary," I said. "I'm an evolutionary."

"That's even worse!"

"Says who?"

"Says they!"

"And what do you care what they think?"

"They won't buy my fish, that's why! I had to take my catch to Hadli twice last week and once already yesterday! Every day now, I don't know which of the fish merchants are going to buy my fish and give me grief for the sorry state of Bree that you singlehandedly wrecked with your childish interest in technology, or if they're going to give me grief and NOT buy my fish at all! *That's* why I care!"

My feelings were so hurt I could have collapsed and cried, but the stronger impulse of anger seized me more fully.

"It's *not* a childish interest! It's *progress*! And I'm not the only one who wants it!" I was hollering like father and hated it. I hated behaving like him. I hated that I was hating at all. "I can't believe I was feeling guilty about leaving you!"

Father glared at me. He wiped his whiskers with his diningcloth and reached for a twig of kono root that Aunt Tala put in a small wooden bowl before she left with Merchant Kam. Every trace of guilt about deserting father to go off to school had left me now. No one but mother knew how tormented I was about abandoning him to his dingy little life in Bree, wifeless, legless, tailless, so impossible a man no woman in her right mind would marry him.

Like the wake that follows a boat in motion, guilt and sadness always left a trail on my International School daydreams. Many nights I laid awake and worried, *if I left for the Continent, what would become of father?* I talked to mother about it and asked her what I should do. I tried to hear her voice, speaking clearly and wisely, but never did. Instead, I imagined what she *might* say to me. The words were typically:

"Go, go to the International Schools. This is *your* life to tend and grow. Your father is still young. Your responsibility to him begins when he's old and feeble. Until then, he's responsible for himself and the life he chooses to live. This is your time, Lin. You are the child. You are the sapling. He had his time when he was a child. Now he's a grown man, capable of taking care of himself. He may find it difficult and a hardship without a wife, but it's in him to tend to himself. This is *your* time, Lin. Don't forget that." Seemed like good advice to me.

In the silence of father's glare, I said, "If I make your life so bad, father, then why not send me away?" He shot me an angry look.

"Seriously, father, maybe that's the best solution. Then you wouldn't have to defend me anymore with all the naysayers."

"I don't want to hear you ever use that word in this house again," father said.

"Which word?"

"Naysayers."

"But they *are* naysayers. What other word can I use?"

"Don't get smart with me."

"Can I say 'the people who are against me'?"

"Lin."

"You're not giving me a choice."

"You don't deserve a choice!"

"What?!"

"*I'm* the father here. You're the child. Let's get that straight."

"Yes," I said, "I *am* the child, and this is *my time*, not yours. You had your time."

"Your time? What kind of nonsense is that?"

"I'm the child, the sapling, this is my time to be nurtured and grown. You had your time, when you were a child. But now it's my time."

"Who's telling you this?" father asked.

"Telling me what?"

"Someone's influencing you with this talk. Who is it?"

"What talk?"

"The sapling! Your time, my time! That talk!"

I said nothing.

"Who, Lin? Who's polluting your mind with these thoughts? Is it Hana?"

Teacher Hana? "No."

"Is it those kids in your club?"

"No!"

"Who, then? Tell me!"

"Why do you care?"

"I need to protect you!"

"I don't need protecting, I need nurturing. I need you to be on my side and help me grow."

"Someone's feeding your mind with these foolish ideas," father squinted and said. "Who is it?"

"I'm not saying."

"I've had enough of your obstinance. Tell me right now or I'll take away your holophone."

"That's not fair!"

"Life's not fair!"

"Just because *your* life's so horribly unfair, doesn't mean you have to make mine miserable!"

Father fell into his angry silence and reached for another twig of kono root. He put the twig in his mouth and spoke in more quiet words, as if already the kono had restored his peace.

"I want to know who," he said, "and I want to know now."

"You won't like who I say."

"I don't care. I want to know."

"It might hurt you and make you sad."

"Just tell me, Lin."

"It's mother."

Father said nothing for the longest time. He didn't move, he didn't blink, he didn't gnaw on his root, he didn't even seem to be breathing. He just sat there like a stone and looked at me with empty eyes.

I said nothing too. What was there to say that could mend this broken moment? I just sat, as still and stoney as him, looking back at him with all the courage I had.

"Your mother, you say?" His voice was soft and emotionless.

"Yes, I talk to her every night before I go to sleep."

Father's eyes grew wide then fell into a squint. "You talk to her?"

"Yes. I tell her the good news of my day. Not just good news of me, but of you and Aunt Tala too. And Teacher Hana, since they're best friends."

"Were."

"What?"

"*Were!*" He pounded his fist. "*Were* best friends! She's not alive, Lin! She can't hear you! And she sure as lightning can't talk to you!"

Of all the cruel words father ever spoke to me, whether he meant them or not, those were the most cruel.

"That's the behavior of a person who's gone mad," he said, "talking to a deceased! I don't know who gave you that idea—"

"Elder Evig's wife did."

"What?! Who's business it is of hers—?"

"She was helping me! I had no one, father! You were grieving and barely spoke to me. Aunt Tala was hardly friendly herself back then. I was lonely and hurting for mother. I missed her so bad, I thought I would die."

Father was silent again, so I said more.

"After service one Adri, the Adri after you disappeared and frightened us and left me feeling like an orphan, I told her I missed mother. She said I could talk to mother in my heart. She said it would help me miss her less. And she was right. Even though I don't talk about mother, I think about her every day. And I talk to her, whether she hears me or not. Mostly at night before I go to sleep, but also in the daytime. Sometimes I just say, 'Hello, mother.' I feel my love for her and I miss her less. You should—"

"Stop!"

"I was going to say, you should try it some time."

"Silence yourself, or I'm taking away everything."

"But—"

"I mean it, Lin! Not another word!"

I took a deep breath. I didn't want to fight with father. Fighting always ended up hurting someone. Tonight, it was hurting father more than me. He was badly bruised, as Aunt Tala would say, and I caused it. Not that I wanted to. I only wanted him to be happy. If I had the power to make him happy, to make him hurt less, to stop him from being angry at everything, I would have. I closed my eyes and asked what love would do with this shipwreck of a conversation.

"Why are your eyes closed?!" father shouted.

"Don't I have the right to close my eyes and reflect?"

"Reflect? What kind of grange belly nonsense is that?"

Oh, no. A dark dread filled me. He said grange belly. The words stung with the pinches of a hundred murtali waterspiders. I hadn't heard him say grange belly in years, not since mother coaxed him out of ever saying it again. It was a spiteful, ugly figure of speech — his invention, his alone.

Father first said grange belly when he came home after his accident, angry and bitter. Since the divers never found his missing leg and tail, father believed that they made it into the belly of the grangefish that tore them from his body. The first time I remember hearing him say grange belly, he had yelled, "What kind of grange belly idea is that?!" I don't remember what the idea was, but he didn't like it. From then on, anytime father was angry, cranky, cross, or frustrated, he'd holler an explosive grange belly expression.

Hearing him say it now was shattering. I stared at my uneaten dinner, fighting the impulse to cry. A tear rolled from my eye and splashed on a kriddlecake.

I looked up at father. "I'm sorry," I said. "I'm really, really sorry." Another tear fell from my bleary eyes.

Father's face softened. He said nothing. We looked at each other, our eyes filling with tears — his eyes, my eyes. I saw a fat tear fall and spill down his cheek. Another fell and another, which he quickly wiped away. But I'd seen them, and I couldn't bear the sight. I buried my face in my diningcloth and cried.

"Father," I sobbed. "I'm so sorry for upsetting you. I never, never want to hurt you."

"You're mumbling," he said. His voice was gentle.

I pressed the diningcloth to my face to soak up the tears. When I opened my eyes, I saw his hand near my plate, palm up. He was reaching for me. I put my hand in his and looked him in the eyes. They were sad and swollen.

"I said, I'm sorry that I upset you. I never want to hurt you."

A tear streamed down his face and hung on a whisker before it fell to his plate and landed on an uneaten kriddlecake. I couldn't help but laugh.

"We're crying in our dinner," I said. "Our tears are falling on our kriddlecakes."

Father half-laughed at the humor. He put his diningcloth to his face. His laughter turned to tears. But he didn't let go my hand, which he lightly held.

Thoughts filled my mind, thoughts that made my heart feel better.

"I usually don't like crying," I said, "but I like crying with you, father. It makes me feel close to you. Like we're in this together."

Though I couldn't see his face, I sensed my words had a soothing effect on him. I saw his whole body lift as he took a long, slow breath. When he exhaled, he let out a soft sigh.

"We love each other, father. And we've both lost the most precious part of our life. We both hurt from the same wound."

Father gripped my hand tight and squeezed his eyes with his diningcloth. His shoulders heaved in small, controlled movements. He was crying again, harder than before.

I wanted to climb in his lap and cry with him. How good it would have felt to cry in each other's arms, as loud and long as we needed and wanted, to cry and cry and cry until every tear was shed. I was too afraid to ask, so I daydreamed it instead, crying together on a gentle sea of love. It was a beautiful daydream, tender and peaceful.

Maybe this was the peace that father had so often wished for. If I could, I would have let all the peace out of me to enter him and be his. In my daydream, I made that happen.

Tell him. The voice was quiet and not words so much as a feeling in my heart. It was a beautiful feeling, full and strong and every- where at once.

In a gentle voice, and as though love were speaking, I told father of my daydream. I told him every part of it, finishing with, "All my peace became yours, father. And even though it's just a daydream, maybe telling you about it will help it be at least a little true."

He had listened to every word, silently crying in his drenched diningcloth, squeezing my hand at certain moments. When I had finished, and after a short silence, he mumbled something.

"What father? I didn't hear you."

He uncovered his face. "I love you, Lin, and I don't want to lose you."

"I don't want to lose you either, father, but I feel like I did a long time ago."

He opened his mouth to speak, but no words came out. He seemed surprised by what I said.

"When I lost mother, I lost you too."

Father squeezed my hand and cleared his throat. "When I lost your mother," he said, "I lost my grip on life. I don't know how to live without her. I don't know how—"

Father released my hand and buried his face in his dining cloth, silently sobbing. I knew by the movement of his back and shoulders.

"I miss her so much," I said. "So, so, so much."

In a mere krillasecond, father snapped and hollered, like a sleeping grandis startled by the pierce of an arrow. "Stop!" he screeched. "Stop right now!"

He glared at me with such intensity I thought I'd catch fire. Where did father's sadness go? What did I say? What did I do?

"What happened, father? Why are you angry at me?"

"Why am I angry at you?" he bellowed. "Why am I angry at you?"

I didn't want him to answer the question, but he did.

"We lost your mother! And what do you do about it? Guilt me into one favor after another like a spoiled child! First the Continental Embassy! I should have never let you go! Do you hear me? I should have never let you go!"

"But it was—"

"It was a mistake! I don't know what they told you there, but I don't like it. I don't like *them!* You came home with your head *filled* with nonsense, and destroyed Bree with it. You want to know why I'm angry at you? You destroyed Bree! There's no peace here! And I sure as a grange belly don't know how we'll ever have peace again! Do you know how serious this is, the mess you made?!"

He stopped his tirade and took a breath and looked at me as if waiting for an answer. I couldn't speak. I just stared at him. At least I had the courage not to look away. In the brief, still silence, I asked what love would do.

"You have no idea, do you," he spewed, "the *mess* you've made! And you want to leave? Run off like a spoiled child having her next round of fun, leaving me with your mess and a ruined reputation? Do you think I'm about to let that happen? Do you?"

Even though I was less afraid, I said nothing. I had heard no voice of love or reason. But I did feel something come over me, and it felt like strength.

"So don't you test me, Lin! You've persisted with me in the past, and I've given in. But I've given in for the last time! Do you hear me? The *last time!* You're all out of favors from me!"

I wasn't about to let this conversation end with a brutal, life-killing ultimatum.

"Father, let's let time help us sort this out."

"No!"

"Won't you at least—?"

"Absolutely not!" Father pounded his fist on the table, stood up and limped to his sleepingroom, his dinner unfinished. That was the last I saw of him until late the next day.

I was hurt and rattled, but not destroyed.

And not discouraged.

Time, my grandmother liked to say, can be your friend or your enemy. It just depends on what you do with it.

I was only ten years old and had nearly two years to make my application to the International Schools. I'd seen what can happen in two weeks and two months. Even two days can turn a person's life around. With two years and a lot of patience, anything could happen.

Time, as I saw it, was on my side.

THE NAYSAYERS

I woke to the sound of shouting — not the angry shout of one person, but the concerned shouts of many. I sat up and trained my ears to the open window of my sleepingroom. There was trouble on Bree Beach.

I leapt to my feet and out the door. "Father? Aunt Tala?"

"Lin!" Aunt Tala was in the kitchen. Her voice was tense with worry.

"Where's father?" I asked.

"He left long ago for fishing."

"Did you hear the shouting? Do you know what's wrong?"

"No, but I'm going to find out." Aunt Tala took a big bite of asi cake.

"I'm coming with you," I said.

"Rorin, usay eur." Aunt Tala had so much cake in her mouth, she garbled every word.

"Your mouth's a mess, Aunt Tala!" I picked up a diningcloth and offered it. "What did you say?"

Aunt Tala took a swig of tichi tea, swallowed hard, and wiped her mouth. "I said, no, Lin, you stay here."

"But Aunt Tala, I want to know what's wrong."

"Then I'll tell you when I return." She picked up her holophone, tossed it in her satchel, and dashed out of the kitchen.

I followed close behind. "If I stay here and wait," I told her, "that's only going to tempt me to disobey you and go anyway."

"Then try not to be tempted." She opened the front door.

"That's impossible to expect of a child!"

She pranced down the eight wooden steps, stopped on the path, and looked up at me. I'd already hopped halfway down.

"All right," she said, "but stay by my side."

As we rushed toward the beach along the Upper Path, I could see the shouters and what they were shouting about. I'd never seen anything like it. A hundred or more odd-looking sea critters were strewn about the sea, floating lifelessly and washing up on the shore.

Someone sped past us on the path.

"Do you know what's wrong?" I asked him.

He turned to answer but kept moving fast. All I heard him say was drowning. I slowed to walking and let Aunt Tala catch up with me.

"What's happening?" she asked.

"There's dead sea critters washing up from the sea. And someone drowned. I don't know who."

When we reached the beach, I ran straight for the shoreline. I stepped on one of the sea critters, slipped on its slimy skin, and fell on my back, landing in a small bed of their dead bodies. I looked closely at one. It wasn't a dead sea critter. It wasn't a critter at all.

"Holophones!" yelled a man who'd just arrived on the scene.

They were holophones.

"Hundreds of them!" the man shouted.

I got to my feet but was too short to see, so I made my way to the Teaching Rock. I hopped up upon it and surveyed the shoreline. He was right. There were hundreds of holophones, in the sea and on the beach. The sight of it was heartbreaking, and were I not so angry, I surely would have cried.

"What happened?" I asked the people standing nearby. "How did this happen, and who—?"

"There she is!" shouted a fisherman in the crowd.

"Who?" someone asked.

"Where?" asked another.

"There! Up on the rock! It's Jorn's girl!"

"It *is* Jorn's girl," said a man's husky voice.

"What should we do with her?"

"I say we jail her! She's a menace to society!"

"You can't jail her for that."

"She's a menace *and* a traitor!" shouted the man with the husky voice. "You sure as thunder can jail her for *that!*" I saw his face in the crowd, staring maniacally at me like a rabid sea raptor.

The ruckus had attracted no small amount of attention. Everyone standing around the Teaching Rock was looking at me now and some not kindly. I saw an open space in the crowd, jumped off the Teaching Rock, and bounded my way through it, back to where I had last seen Aunt Tala. The crowd was thick and tall enough to hide me from the pointing people, and I felt safe from harm.

"Aunt Tala!" I yelled in search of her. "Aunt Tala!" I hopped up high in hopes I would see her. "Aunt Tala!"

There was no sight of her. I stood and stared in disbelief at the holophones floating in the sea. One of them washed up over my foot and rested there. I picked it up and inspected it carefully. *Indestructible,* I thought. It was in no way damaged.

"Tried to drown 'em," said a man close behind me. "But the monstrosities won't sink!"

A naysayer! I kept my back to him, so I could listen unrecognized.

"Got to burn them," said one of his naysayer friends.

"We tried to burn them," said another.

"Tried?"

"Yep, won't burn either."

"What save stone won't burn?"

"Got me," said a voice I knew. Fisher Brae, old and long retired.

"That's the problem with foreign-made things," said the first naysayer. "Don't know what you're dealing with."

"We got a mighty force on our hands."

"A mighty force to reckon with."

"It's these people," said Fisher Brae. "These Continentals. *They're* the force to be reckoned with."

"Don't even start with that dimwit idea. They've got an army that could level Bree in a day."

"Yep, he's right. Don't mess with the Continentals. We need to take care of the problem right here at home."

"I know a way we can sink them," said the first naysayer. "A brilliant idea. Just thought of it."

"Then tell us then."

"We've got to sink them with stones. Put them in a washingbag with some stones inside, throw it overboard, and there! Never see them again."

"Jin, that *is* brilliant."

"All right, fellas, let's gather up these grange belly abominations before the others get to them. Loel, I'll take that extra satchel."

Grange belly? That's father's phrase! Father's phrase and his alone. Was he in on this? My broken heart broke more.

"Hey, is that that girl?"

"What girl?"

"Jorn's girl!"

"It *is* Jorn's girl!"

I ducked down low, looked for an opening in the crowd, and ran all the way home.

***

"There you are!" Aunt Tala said when she arrived nearly an hour later. I was curled up on a cushion in our sittingroom. "Lin, are you all right?"

"No, I'm terrible."

She sat down by my side and softly rubbed my back. "You know, then."

"I heard it straight from the mouths of some naysayers. They did this on purpose, Aunt Tala."

"I know, sweetness, I know."

I shifted and nestled my head in her lap. She gently scratched the space between my ears, just the way I taught her to when I was having nightmares.

"Thanks, Aunt Tala. You feel like mother. It's nice."

"School's called off for the day," she said.

"Then what am I going to do all day?"

"Your grandparents say they'd like to see more of you. You could spend the day with them."

"Ordinarily, I would, but I'm in a fragile state."

Aunt Tala laughed. "Fragile state? Where'd you hear that from?"

"My holophone. I found some information on losing a loved one. It said that the death of a mother can leave a child in a fragile state for a long time."

"These holophones, Lin." Aunt Tala clacked her tongue in a show of disapproval.

"Why'd you say it like that?"

"They're causing so much trouble."

"But you're still glad you have one, aren't you?"

"Yes," she said, "I am. But they're still trouble."

"The naysayers are the trouble."

"They're *part* of the trouble," Aunt Tala said. "They don't get all the blame."

"Then what's the other part of the trouble?"

"Their incessant use."

"What does that mean?"

"It means these holophones are taking over the lives of our children, and a lot of parents aren't happy about it."

"Why?"

"Look around you, Lin. Every child who has a holophone is obsessed with it, wearing it day and night. Wearing it at school, at the dinner table, wearing it to bed."

"But they just got them," I said, "Of course they'll be obsessed. It'll wear off after a while."

"How long is a while, though? And in the meantime, what kind of habits are going to set in?"

"Aunt Tala, whose side are you on?"

She was silent for a moment. "I'm on everyone's side, Lin. I want this to work for everyone."

"So do I."

"I know you do."

"I think father may be in on it," I said.

"In on what?"

"The naysayers' plan to destroy the holophones."

"What makes you think that?"

"I heard some of them talking on the beach," I told her. "One of them said grange belly."

"Grange belly?"

"You never heard father say that?"

"No," she nodded.

"It's a saying father invented," I said, "a long time ago. Mother made him quit. And he did until now. No one else would know to say grange belly unless they talked to father and heard him say it."

"That doesn't make him guilty of their crimes. He could have said that to them anytime."

"You think so?"

"I'm quite positive."

"Oh." Maybe father wasn't in on it. I hoped so. "You might be right, Aunt Tala. Still, it hurt my feelings to hear them say it."

"Well, that should be no surprise. You are, after all, in a fragile state." She laughed, hoping I would laugh with her, but I didn't. She love-tugged my ear and said, "I have an idea."

Her idea was supremely great. She called Merchant Kam, explained the situation, and asked if I could come to work with her that day.

"Of course," he replied.

A warm stream of happiness filled my fragile state with strength and hope. And just like that, my whole day changed.

LOVE'S WISDOM

They had work to do, Merchant Kam and Aunt Tala, so I entertained myself with my holophone in Merchant Kam's office. I nestled in a big, bowled puffy chair and called Mira.

"The person you called is not powered on at this time," said the voice of my holophone, a kind woman's voice that I picked from thirty choices. She sounded the most like mother. "Do you wish to record a communication?"

"Yes," I said. "Mira, look where I am! You'll never guess, 'cause you've never been here. It's Merchant Kam's office. Were you at the beach today? Did you hear what happened? I was there and saw it all. Some naysayers tried to sink hundreds of holophones—you know, the extra ones that the Continentals left behind. They're going to try and drown them again. A man named Jin's behind it. I already told Merchant Kam what happened, and he said he'd tell the Mayor. I don't understand, Mira. Why are they against progress and technology? Why do they want to miss out on the greatest fun ever invented? If they only knew what they were missing, they'd change their minds…. So, where are you? I can't believe I'm talking to you through a machine! Did you know that my voice is going all the way to the Forton satellite to get to your holophone? I feel happy just thinking about that. I wish I could talk to you with you talking back. A conversation just isn't the same without two people…. Well," I said, lonely and hurting, "I miss you. Call me when you power on…. Message complete."

I tried my best to shake off my sadness, leaned back in Merchant Kam's massive softwood chair with double thick cushions, and started to drift into a daydream of working for Merchant Kam and traveling the world on important business. Then I realized I *could* travel the world on my holophone. The lifeless daydream disappeared from my mind like a pebble dropped in the sea.

"Flight," I commanded. "Depart present location...."

I was flying over Swef, the capitol city of Orilon, when my holophone sounded three short tweeps in ascending tonals. That was the tweep/tonal combination that meant someone was calling me.

"Terminate flight," I said. The tall buildings and modern homes of the enormous city of Swef disappeared. "Show me who's calling." An image of Mira appeared, sitting in her sleepingroom at her house, her kipper-paper notebook in her lap. She was smiling.

"Mira," I said, "where've you been today?"

"First the beach," she said, "then the Mayor's Office."

"Why were you at the Mayor's Office?"

"He had a meeting. All the school officials were there and some of the Village Council and the Committee of Technology—"

"The Committee of Technology?"

"Yes, not all of them," she said, "three I think. Father had to be there and agreed to take me with him. I sat outside the Mayor's Office. I sat close to the door and wrote down everything they said."

"I want to hear it all."

Mira tapped her chin with her kipper-ink pen. "If I were to give the meeting a book title," she said, "it would be *The Great Holophone Menace of 2294*." We shared a short, paltry laugh. The word menace wasn't so funny anymore. "Seriously, though," she said, "there's big trouble brewing."

"What kind of trouble?"

"Everyone's complaining about the holophones."

"Not everyone."

"Way more than you think," she said. "More than you want to know."

My throat tightened. I felt a long trissilfish wrap around my neck twenty times, which actually happened to me once in a nightmare. It was the same sensation as in the dream, which made everything Mira was about to say even more painful.

"The school officials aren't happy that students are coming to class with their holophones. They called it a perilous distraction from teaching and learning. They said the teachers don't want any holophones in class. Ever."

"Ever?"

"Ever. The School Council's going to vote on that next week. But that's not all," she said. "The Village Council members talked about complaints from people in their districts. You wouldn't believe what some people are worried about. I'll read you some," Mira looked down at her kipper-paper notebook and read from her notes. "Some people think the Continentals are spying on us through our holophones. Some think that holophones will rot the brain. Some think the whole town will become corrupted by the bad influence of other cultures. Some worry that all the kids of Bree will want to move away to other places they see, thinking they'll be happier there. Then someone said, 'These holophones are going to bring the death of Bree, take it right off the map'. Not sure what they meant by that. Then someone else said, 'Maybe that's what they want.'." Mira looked up at me. "I think they mean the Continentals."

"They're blaming the Continentals," I said.

"Yes, but worse, they're making up nonsense stories about our holophones. I heard the entire meeting, and no one said, 'Well, that's pretty farfetched.' No one, not even my father. They just talked like everything that was said was true."

"I can't believe this is happening, Mira."

Mira shook her head. "Me neither."

"I don't understand, everyone was so happy about this."

"Not everyone's unhappy," she said.

"Then why aren't *they* talking?"

"I guess it's only the complainers who take the trouble to talk."

"I think the naysayers are poisoning people's minds."

"Oh, and about that," Mira said.

"What?"

"The naysayers formed a group. They're calling themselves the *Preservationaries.*"

"A group like ours?"

"Yep."

"Is preservationaries a word?"

"No, but neither is evolutionaries."

"Oh…. But, so what, right? The naysayers are a small minority."

"They *were* small when we were doing the petition," Mira said, "but now there are more."

"Mira, that frightens me."

"Me too."

I saw a tear fall from her eye. My whole body throbbed with an unpleasant pain.

"I don't understand it," I said. "Why do adults have to complicate everything? Why does life have to be so unfair and hurt everyone so much? Father cried last night, right in front of me."

"Your father cried?"

"Yes, we cried together. Want to hear the story?"

"Absolutely."

I told Mira about Merchant Kam's visit and what he said to father about the International Schools and how father and I ate alone and argued and shouted, but then cried together, but then he got angry again and shouted some more. Mira loved that we cried. It was her favorite part of the story.

"I haven't seen him all day, Mira. After what happened today, I don't know what kind of mood he's going to be in. I'm scared to see him."

"That's bad," she said. "What are you going to do?"

"I don't know. I want to do what love would do, but when I'm afraid, the voice of love is impossible to hear."

"I wish I had some advice for you."

"Lin, there you are." It was Aunt Tala's voice. She was standing close.

"I'm talking to Mira!" I told her. "She's at her house, and I'm here, and we're talking! Isn't that—?"

"Yes, but you better get off."

"What's wrong?"

"I need to talk to you."

"Is it bad?"

"You won't like it."

The trissilfish tightened again around my neck. Even though it was imagined, I still couldn't breathe.

"What's—?"

"*Now*, Lin. Say goodbye."

"Mira, you heard it, something bad's happened. I'll tell you about it later. Got to go."

"I'm rooting for you Lin, whatever it is."

"Thanks, Mira, you're the best."

"*Lin.*"

"All right, Aunt Tala."

"Bye, Mira." I cleared my throat. "Terminate the call, please."

"Call terminated," my holophone said, "thank you."

I thought of mother, took off my holophone, and followed Aunt Tala down the softstone hallway to Merchant Kam's office, the trissilfish tightening with every step.

"Your father's been arrested," Aunt Tala said. "He's being held in jail."

"Arrested? Why? What'd he do?"

"I'm not sure of the details, but he's been charged with sedition."

"What's that?"

"It's like treason."

"You mean traitor treason?"

"I don't know, Lin. It's ludicrous, if you ask me." She was angry and not at me.

"What do we do, Aunt Tala?"

194

"I don't know, Lin, I don't know."

"What would love do?"

"What?"

"We need to ask what love would do."

"Lin, this is serious!"

"I *am* being serious! The best way to solve our problems is to ask what love would do." Aunt Tala glared at me. I told her, "Elder Evig's wife said that. *She* can't be wrong!"

We entered Merchant Kam's office. He was standing near the door, calm and smiling.

"Tala, she's right," he said. "Especially in times of crisis, we do well to seek love's wisdom."

Though the office was small, Aunt Tala kept walking, pacing along one side of the room.

"How can you say that, Kam?" she said. "Love can't get Jorn out of jail. This is a crisis, and in times of crisis, we need *action — practical action.*"

"We need both," Merchant Kam said. "Love *and* action. Ideally in that order. And don't be concerned, Tala. I've already taken action."

Aunt Tala stopped pacing. "Oh?"

"I just spoke with Constable Bue. I'm on my way there now, to the lock-up where Jorn's being held."

"Good," she said, "I'm going with you."

"Me, too," I said, eager for the adventure. I'd never been to the jail before.

Merchant Kam shook his head. "You two stay here. Lin might be in danger."

My eyes grew wide and I nearly smiled. "Danger?"

"The Constable said there's an agitated mob outside the jail."

"The naysayers," I said. I looked at Aunt Tala. "Merchant Kam's right. There'd be danger for me there. And you too, probably. You're father's sister."

Aunt Tala clacked her tongue. "These holophones, Lin."

Her words made me angry, not at her, but at adults generally and me too, for that matter. All this blaming! The naysayers blamed father. Father blamed me. I blamed the naysayers. Aunt Tala blamed the holophones. And a lot of people were blaming the Continentals. That left Merchant Kam. Who did he blame?

"Stay here," he said as he turned to the door. "Keep your holophones powered-on. I'll call you when I know something."

I leapt and slid across the smoothtile floor to block his passage at the door. I had questions for Merchant Kam.

"But what about love?" I asked him. "I want to know what love would do in this crisis."

"Just what you're doing, Lin. Love would be calm. Love would trust. Love would choose the best choice our practical mind offers, even if it's not the choice you want."

"What do you mean?"

"You wanted to go with me to the jail," he said, "but I told you to stay here. You would have rather gone, but you chose to stay, without a fight, without a fuss. That's what love would do. Give up what you wanted for what was best."

"Is that how love and practicality work together?"

"Yes, that's one way."

"You're supremely smart," I said.

He smiled. "I had a supremely excellent education."

"The International Schools?"

"Yes. And life."

"I have lots of questions about the International Schools," I said. "Can I talk to you about them sometime?"

"Yes, Lin," he nodded, "I would enjoy that." He kissed the top of my head and said to me quietly, "You're stronger than you know."

I closed my eyes and daydreamed that the kiss and words were father's.

"Don't worry," I heard him say to Aunt Tala. "Everything's going to be all right." He squeezed her hand and left us.

"I think you should marry him," I whispered without thinking.

Aunt Tala smiled but said nothing.

"He's a wonderful man and he cares about us," I said. "I think in a certain way, he loves us. You, me, even father."

Aunt Tala looked at me, her face soft. "Maybe so."

"He's a lot like a Continental."

"I suppose he is."

"Father's going to be mad at me for a long time, but I'm not afraid."

"Not right now."

"Don't spoil it, Aunt Tala."

"I don't mean to spoil your fearlessness, Lin. I'm just being realistic."

"Fearlessness. I like that, Aunt Tala. That's something love would do. Be fearless."

Fearless.

Fearless. Fearless. Fearless.

Fearless became my new favorite word, a trusty friend and weapon in the fights I would have to fight.

It was true, big trouble was brewing in Bree, and the trouble was just beginning.

Extras

Glossary

ADIBADI The distant ancestral cousin of the people of Luratia. Adibadis are to Luratians what the chimpanzee is to the humans of Earth, though they more closely resemble the domesticated dog in their character and temperament. Adibadis are loyal companions and excellent workers — easily trainable, eager to please, happy to serve. They are gentle playmates of children and loving members of the families with whom they live.

ADRI The sixth day of Luratia's 6-day week.

ALTERON One of the Continent's two super-satellites, a city in the sky. In addition to collecting and transmitting solar power to Luratia, Alteron is a fully equipped base for excursions to space. It is home, at any given time, to as many as 48 residents.

ARGEN An archaic coin, used only in the extreme southeastern region of the continent of Wershonia, the land of Lin's birthplace. World-wide there are less than a dozen coined and paper currencies still in use, having been displaced by hundreds of cryptocurrencies. This number grows every year.

ARTUNNE The largest of Luraita's six continents and the epicenter of its recent technological and social awakening. The nine nations of Artunne unified as a single sovereign country 158 years ago, which evolved after decades of reconstruction following the catastrophic

Asteroid Shear of 2096. Two million lives were lost in the tragedy, but a remarkable period of cooperative rebuilding and technological innovation was inspired.

ASI A nutty grain similar to buckwheat. It grows so widely and easily almost every family in Southern Wershonia has a thicket of it in their yard. Asi is highly nutritious. It's one of the first solid foods infants are fed; it is one of the few foods the aged and ailing can eat.

BISRI The first day of Luratia's 6-day week.

BREE Lin's birthplace; a small, primitive fishing village in the country of Strellin on the southeast coast of the continent of Wershonia.

CELERWOX The fastest animal in the world. A sleek, 4-legged mammal, thin, light-boned, and very muscular.

CEMENOT A flower that grows low to the ground and self-protectively closes up when an animal or person approaches.

CLARKON An organic and incredibly versatile "super-material" known on Earth as graphene It is the first 2D material ever discovered and is used in thousands of applications. Learn more about clarkon on page 221.

CONTINENT The nation-continent of Artunne, whose nine countries unified as a single sovereign nation 158 years ago.

DELORIA The most beautiful of the six continents of Luratia. Dry crops grow in the South and wet crops grow in the North. Its southern beaches are popular tourist destinations due to the powdery violet sand and occasionally sunny patches of sky. The people of Deloria are simple and happy, which some believe is due to their exceptionally good weather.

EGLI The smallest of Luratia's six continents. Egli is rich in minerals, precious stones, and a crystalline substance once used for fuel. For thousands of years this land has been mined with slave labor. Egli has no countries, but is divided into four sectors that are governed by the majority landowners. Coastal cities and ports are the only vestige of civilization here.

FORTON The smaller of Luratia's two super-satellites. Like the Alteron satellite platform, Forton collects and transmits solar power to the planet, which is then wirelessly distributed world-wide.

GOSTIN One of Luratia's six continents. Gostin is so rainy, most of its cities are covered by invisible, self-repairing clarkon nets that shield rain and lightning. Rain falls almost continuously in the northern mountains, which nourishes the growth of medicinal mosses that are exported all over the world. Though they are not as wealthy as Continentals or Wershonians, the people of Gostin enjoy a very high standard of living.

GRANDIS The largest animal in Wershonia. Four-legged, bowled back, carnivorous, shy but mean. Everyone knows never to sneak up on a grandis, they don't like surprises. Fortunately, they don't run very fast.

GRANGEFISH A large predatory fish unsuitable for eating due to its extremely unpleasant taste and texture. Grangefish have three rows of upper teeth and two rows of lower teeth that interlock when the mouth is closed. The jaw of the grangefish is so strong, it requires three grown men to pry it open. It was a grangefish that took Lin's father's leg and tail while he fought it underwater with his bare hands.

GROILE A type of grassy moss that grows on in the tropical regions of the Continent. Groile is soft and free of feeders and insects since no living creature can bear its intensely pungent taste. Patches of groile serve as seating areas wherever they are found: on private lawns, in public parks, on school grounds, in outdoor amphitheatres.

HODRI The fourth day of Luratia's 6-day week.

HOLOPHONE Luratia's HD virtual-reality smartphone is capable of holographic transmission and projection, simulated flight (across the planet or out into space), augmented reality (data overlays), and access to the holographic World Library (a virtual-reality wikipedia).

INTERNATIONAL SCHOOLS Three international boarding schools for gifted teenagers of Luratia, located on island campuses of the Continent. These schools without classrooms are experience-based and emphasize teamwork, communication skills, vocational training, and world travel both real and virtual.

KIPPER A fantastically slimy purple seaplant that is used for many purposes among the people of Southern Wershonia: the liquid is used for dye and ink, the pulp is used to make paper, the dried leaves are salted and eaten as a snack, and the wet leaves, when held tight, can be used as a whistle.

KODRI The third day of Luratia's 6-day week.

KONO ROOT A prized root plant that grows abundantly in the equatorial regions of the planet. The extract is used as an anesthesia. The dried root, chewed or drunk as tea, is a calming sedative.

KULI A small port city west of Bree on the southern coast of Wershonia. Offshore, about 10 Earth miles south of the coast, is an embassy of the Continent, located on a man-made island. Kuli is the hub of watertravel to the Continental Embassy from the mainland of Wershonia.

LURATIA A cloudy, solar-powered planet roiling in the wonders and hazards of its Nano Age (as Earth soon will). This is a time of explosive developments in technology, energy production, warfare, communication, and in some places, social maturity. But progress on Luratia, as on most civilizing worlds, is grossly uneven. The remote village of Bree — Lin's birthplace and the setting of this story — has been untouched by the new technologies so rapidly advancing elsewhere in the world. The mining operations on the continent of Egli still owns it workers, the last slave race of Luratia.

LURATIANS Luratians stand on average five feet high. They have two legs, a long muscular tail, and two hands with four long fingers sandwiched between two thumbs. They have round eyes with large pupils and cat-like ears. Recent generations in the advanced countries of the world have been tweaked by genetic engineering, which has proved both beneficial and disastrous.

MISRI The second day of Luratia's 6-day week.

MURTALI A small, poisonous waterspider. While murtali venom is not lethal, it paralyzes the victim for several hours. It was a murtali bite that caused the death of Lin's mother while swimming in the Strellin Sea.

NADRI The second day of Luratia's 6-day week.

STRELLIN A nation of Wershonia, one of two that make up Southern Wershonia. Lin's native country.

SUB-ORBITAL AIRBUS A rocket-propelled craft that traverses long distances in a short time by ascending to a very high altitude and arcing in the direction of its destination. For coast-to-coast flights on the Continent, the sub-orbital airbus achieves an altitude of 50 Earth miles above sea level. For oceanic voyages, the altitudinal lift peaks at 80 miles, which provides passengers a view of Luratia that only their astronauts know.

TICHI   The large, lightweight seeds of the tichi bush are used to stuff cushions for sleeping and sitting.

TRISSILFISH Trissilfish have no teeth, no eyes, nor a front or back side. They are an ancient simple-cell fish. Any part of their long string-like body can eat the invisibly small microbial creatures they feed on. A single strand of trissilfish can grow as long as the combined height of two men, and their stringy bodies weave and tangle to form nests containing as many as 2,000 individual trissils.

TURO BIRD   A domesticated bird raised for food. A large turo bird farm operates in West Bree.

VOLO FISH   These graceful, playful fish swim near boats and like to frolic in their wake. Volo fish leap out of the water to snatch mid-air the low-flying bugs they feed on.

VONA   One of 20 islands that dot the perimeter of the Continent and one of 3 islands that are home to the campuses of the International Schools, boarding schools for gifted teenagers from all parts of the world.

WATURI   One of the 6 continents of Luratia. Waturi is a small continent with a large population, due to its crowded coastal cities and high birth rates. The interior of Waturi is desolate and rich in natural geysers. The entire coastline, by contrast, is nearly one continual mega-city, demarcated by the boundaries of 3 nations, who are embroiled in disputes over water rights and other natural resources. The nations of Waturi are significant stakeholders in mining operations on Egli, a short distance away.

WERSHONIA   Luratia's second largest continent. A wide and steep mountain range separates the North from South, which made land travel between them nearly impossible until the invention of aircraft. Learn more about Wershonia on page 228.

WILD MOUNTAIN BEREK   This 6-legged mountain beast is incredibly agile on steep rock. Unlike the grandis, bereks are very social creatures. They mate for life and roam in clans. They're indisputably ugly and eat just about anything, making them the most omni of all omnivores native to Wershonia. While the flesh of the berek is inedible, a highly prized cheese is made of their fat.

CLARKON, AKA GRAPHENE

Though this book is fiction,

C L A R K O N   I S   R E A L.

Earth scientists call it **graphene.**

They call it the "miracle material".

Have you ever heard a scientist describe

anything as miraculous?

As it has on Luratia,

graphene is changing life on Earth

in **new** and **big** and **extraordinary** ways.

What makes graphene so extraordinary? ››

10 Amazing Facts about Graphene

1. Graphene is **100 times stronger than steel** of the same thickness and **many times lighter**.

2. If a **piece of paper** the length of a **football field** were as strong and stiff as graphene, you could hold it at one end with **no breaking or bending**.

3. You could hold that 100-yard piece of paper **with just two fingers**.

4. A sheet of graphene as **thick as plastic wrap** would support the **weight of an elephant**.

5. A square yard could hold **a 10-pound cat** and would weigh no more than **a whisker**.

6. Graphene **electrons move 100–10,000 times faster** than silicon electrons. That means computer chips will soon go warp speed *and* get smaller.

7. Graphene **kills bacteria**, even the dreaded E. coli.

8. Graphene **makes energy from** any wavelength of light, even **light we can't see**.

9. Graphene is so strong you can **hold a 1-atom-thick sheet** of it **with your own hands**.

10. **And that's what graphene is:** a 1-atom-thick sheet of carbon atoms, which makes it **a 2-dimensional material**.

See for yourself ››

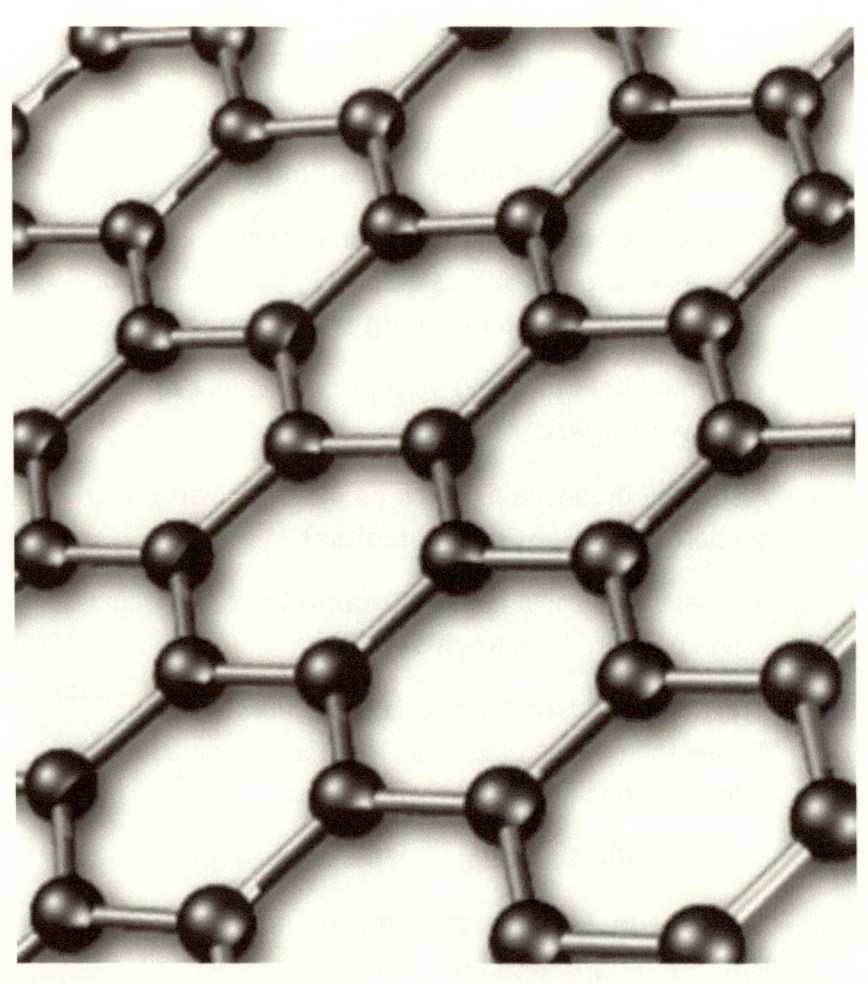

the fat dots are carbon atoms
the lines are the bonds between them

**Graphene is about to change life on Earth
in big and extraordinary ways ›***

EARTH'S FUTURE, COURTESY OF GRAPHENE

Self-powering devices — no batteries, no cords. The secret is a **graphene coating** that **makes power** as it's needed from the **smallest bits** of **nearby light**.

Super-huge, paper-thin, light-weight computer screens that **roll up** like a poster for easy transport.

Computer nanochips that could store a **terabyte** or more on a chip the size of a **grain of salt**.

Buildings that are **fireproof, lightning-proof,** and **earthquake-proof**.

Vehicles with **photovoltaic paint** that **supplies power,** even on cloudy days.

Pocket-size water purification devices that turn the dirtiest, saltiest water into **100% pure H_2O**.

Clothing that continuously **monitors** a person's **blood pressure**.

Storage containers that **keeps food fresh for weeks and months**, not days and days.

Smart biomaterials that can **detect disease**.

Space elevators! Made of **super-strong, self-powering graphene cables** that stretch from the surface of Earth to an orbiting satellite.

Wershonia

A wide and steep mountain range separates the North from South, which made land travel between them nearly impossible until the invention of aircraft. Much of the steep, rocky coast north of Bree is uninhabited by people and this further restricted travel between the North and South along the eastern coast.

While much of Southern Wershonia is still steeped in ancient traditions and olden ways, Northern Wershonia has been modernizing for centuries. It ranks second in the world on almost every measurable metric: quality of life, longevity, gender and race equality, technological progress, educational excellence, economic health, and political stability.

Directly south of the port town of Kuli is a man-made island where an embassy of the Continent is located. It was established as a central organizing hub for the many humanitarian service projects it supports throughout this region of the world. It houses medical facilities, a holographic World Library, and mediation services for conflict resolution. This is one of three Embassy Islands in the world, and each is located nearest the least developed nations, where humanitarian need is greatest and the ability to travel long distances is most difficult.

THE CONTINENT OF WERSHONIA

OF THE PLANET LURATIA

the
Continent
(Artunne)

ALGALON

ORILON

SIMILON

Tilani Sea

NORTHERN WERSHONIA

STRELLIN

SOUTHERN WERSHONIA

Bree

Waturi
Gostin
Deloria

TOBBS

Kuli

Strellin Sea

Egli

Embassy Island

THE LURATIAN YEAR

dry season	1	BISO	freedom months, no school
	2	MISA	
	3	KOSO	
	4	HO	
wet season	5	NASO	school months
	6	ASO	
	7	RASA	
	8	TA	THE 10 MONTHS OF A LURATIAN YEAR
	9	OSA	
dry	10	RO	

A Luratian year is 299 and a half days. Thousands of years ago the smarter of Lin's ancestors made a 10-month year of 30 days each to mark the passage of time.

1 year = 10 months = 300 days (299.423 to be exact)

1 month = 5 weeks = 30 days

1 week = 6 days

1 day = 20 hours

THE LURATIAN MONTH

Koso 2293

Bisri	Misri	Kodri	Hodri	Nadri	Adri
1	2	3	4	5	6
7	8	9	10	11	12
13	14	15	16	17	18
19	20	21	22	23	24
25	26	27	28	29	30

Luratian months are 30 days long and conveniently identical: same days, same dates.

If it's the 10th, you always know it's Hodri.

Adri is their Sunday. Bisri is their Monday.

Luratians call Nadri "Half Day", a day of half-work or school and half-play.

ALBEREO AND THE PHENOMENON
OF BINARY STARS

Albereo (spelled Albireo by some) is one of the most beautiful double stars in the visible universe. It is made up of a small blue star and a large golden yellow star. Since they sparkle like brilliant jewels when viewed through a telescope, astronomers refer to their color as sapphire and topaz.

From a distance, a binary star looks like a single star but really it is two stars, paired up for billions and billions of years, locked in a gravitational embrace from which they never waver. The two stars are often of different mass and size, but still they remain joined in perfect equilibrium. You might be amazed to know that most stars in the universe are binary.

Stars grow bigger and hotter as they grow old, and the eventual death of a star is not a quiet passing — some stars expire with a massive supernova explosion. Each star in a binary pair evolves in this way, but they do so at different rates. When one star grows so big that its mass begins to endanger the life of its companion, it transfers its mass to the smaller star. The death-explosion of the larger star is delayed, often for millions or billions of years. By giving part of itself to the other, the larger star lengthens the lives of both. It is a demonstration of a beautiful truth of kindness: *when one shares unselfishly, all will benefit — even eventually the one who gave.*

About the Author

Melanie Pahlmann is a journalist, editor, love advocate, and ardent optimist. She believes that Earth's best years are ahead of us, despite the dystopian futures that haunt our storytelling. Some may call her views utopian, but she disagrees. Decency, wisdom, and cooperation aren't impossible achievements, not for a person and not for a world.

Melanie is a backyard astronomer and lives in southern Arizona, where the night sky is very dark, rarely cloudy, and stunningly starry.

To learn more about Lin's world and amazing graphene
and to contact Melanie, please visit

www.luratia.com

the exoplanetary life of Lin of Luratia

BOOK 1
how to be happy on a cloudy planet

BOOK 2
thank you and happy flying

BOOK 3
pure sky life